Together Again..........I Promise

By

Linda Salinas

1

Copyright © 2019 Linda Salinas

ISBN-13: 9781794439375

To

Albert and Carla

Acknowledgments

I want to thank Robin Munro, the friend and parent of one of my students who spent time with me to explain how she wrote and published her first book. She took me step by step through the initial process and explained how easy it is with the program CreateSpace/KDP Amazon. When I ran into a glitch, she took the time to send me a phone number where I could get immediate help. With her help, I was able to get one book published and now this second one. As I am learning, I am very willing to help others to enjoy the fun of writing and publishing.

I also want to thank my husband, Albert, who sits many nights in front of the television, while I type incessantly on my books. Thankfully, the click—click—click of the keyboard gets drowned out by the tv.

I also want to thank the many friends who read my first book and gave me a much-welcomed critique. That response gave me the initiative to write this second book.

And finally, thanks to my mother for being my mother.

Together Again....I Promise

Chapter 1
Young Love

It was April. The schoolyear was coming to an end. Julie was excited to complete her junior year at the high school and spend some time doing all of the fun things that high school girls do in the summer: sun tanning, swimming, shopping, gossiping, hanging out with friends, and *maybe* a little work! She had a fairly packed schedule academically, plus Julie played volleyball and ran track. It was grueling at times, so a change of schedule was certainly welcomed.

Julie was a beautiful seventeen-year-old girl with a fun and bubbly personality. Julie's mother, Gloria, was a wonderful homemaker who also worked as a seamstress when she could fit it into her family's schedule. Her father, Randell, was very hard-working. He worked for a company that manufactured train parts and equipment. He had worked his way up, beginning as a low-level worker when he was only sixteen, to the position he held now. Without a college degree, he didn't think he could hold a management position, but he was a great worker and was respected by everyone in the company.

Julie knew the value of hard work and never took her parents for granted. She knew they sacrificed throughout the years to provide for her and her brother.

They lived in a very modest house, but it was completely paid for; there was no mortgage. Her father believed in living within one's means, so he never bought things on credit. He paid cash for what was needed. If they didn't have the money on hand, they waited until they did. He didn't believe in insurance. He didn't have insurance on the house or any of the car other than the mandatory liability insurance. He believed that if something happened to the house or one of the cars, he would just buy another house or buy another car. He was optimistic that nothing would happen. He also was very handy and could fix almost anything. He knew electrical systems, plumbing systems, and a little air conditioning. He believed you should do everything yourself. Calling a plumber or an electrician was out of the question, unless the job was so difficult that he didn't know how to handle it himself. Even then, he asked a friend who may know how to fix the situation. He also instilled in his kids the idea that they could do anything---*anything.* So, because of that, Julie thought she could do anything---could fix anything---could make anything.

"Bye, Mom!" Julie yelled as she ran out the front door for school. "I'll be in a little late today, because I'm meeting some of my friends at the Dairy Queen. We are having a committee meeting there, believe it or not! Really, we do have to get some work done for the end of the year party coming up."

"OK, Julie---be careful," her mother answered. She never had to worry about Julie. Julie was mature for her age, and she was totally responsible. They had a great relationship, too.

Julie bounced down the sidewalk. Long, blonde curls cascaded down from her black, velvet headband. Her hair now reached below her shoulders, because she had been too busy to even get it trimmed. She usually resorted to just trimming her hair herself. She knew it wasn't the best home cut, but it had worked for many years and no one ever said anything about it.
It was still chilly outside in the mornings so she wore a soft, cream-colored sweater to top her pink and cream plaid skirt.

Julie's mother watched as Julie climbed into her car. *I'm such a lucky mother*, Gloria thought to herself. *I have such a beautiful and intelligent daughter who is as pretty on the inside as she is on the outside. I'm blessed.*

Gloria was certainly correct. Besides Julie being a beautiful young woman, she was genuinely kind and considerate. She respected everyone, from the housekeepers and janitors who worked in her father's office to the teachers and administrators who worked at her high school. She loved everyone and everyone loved her.

Chapter 2
Coincidental Meeting

Arriving at the Dairy Queen around the same time, eight girls piled out of three cars and headed through the front door. They walked straight to the large table at the back of the restaurant---you could tell they had been there before.

"Ok, girls," Julie said, calling the unofficial meeting to order. "We've got to come up with a really good party this year. This is our last chance to really make an impact on the underclassmen!"

"Agreed!" they chimed in.

"Julie, let's have a better menu this time around. Can we get some ideas from our local restaurants? They are the real experts. They know students are poor, too, so they will try to keep the cost low," one of the girls offered.

"Absolutely!" Julie replied. "OK, you take that on, alright?"

"What about the location? I know we always have it in the school gym, but isn't there some place else that we can consider?" Mary inquired as she folded a paper napkin into a small bird. She loved origami.

"I agree with you totally!" Julie answered. "I'll be happy to ask some other places if they can accommodate our group."

As the meeting progressed, one by one the other girls took on duties to perform, all with the goal of making this party the best ever.

They had also ordered by this time, and their food was being delivered. There was almost a fight in the kitchen. The local high school boys who worked there were fighting over WHO would be the one to deliver the food to the big table in the rear of the restaurant. Who wouldn't want to take the orders to eight absolutely beautiful girls! And these boys were in the tenth grade, so they were in total awe!

The girls laughed and giggled so much that the entire place was feeling happy. Other people in the restaurant laughed---not at what was being said because they didn't know---but they laughed because the girls' laughter was so funny. It was contagious!

Finally, the official planning committee and fun-loving social committee was finished. The last French-fry was consumed and the last sip of chocolate shake was finished. The girls got up, grabbed their purses and notebooks that contained their valuable planning notes and headed for the front door.

"Thank you!" the girls chimed in as they looked toward the group of young boys who were watching every step they took.

"No----THANK YOU!" the boys yelled back in unison. Then everyone laughed loudly.

"Hey girls---you all go on----I want to thank the manager," Julie called out to the others as they exited.

2

The girls walked out the door, but Julie turned around to walk to the counter where the manager was standing.

"Thank you so much for everything," she said to the tall, lanky college boy who managed the Dairy Queen. "Your servers were super. I hope we weren't too loud with all of our laughter."

With that, she turned and headed to the door. Before she could open the door, someone opened it from the outside for her. A tall, very handsome young man waited for her to walk through the door.

"Oh! Thank you so very much. I really appreciate that!" Julie said looking the young man directly in the eye. *Wow! I think that is the most handsome man I have ever seen in my life!* She thought.

"My pleasure!" he replied. Julie didn't know it, but he felt the very same way. He had seen many, many beautiful girls, but something about her was very, very different. He couldn't put his finger on it, but there was something there. *I really need to find out who she is. Make a mental note,* he thought.

Julie got in her car. He glanced out the window and made a note that her car was an older-model, black Ford sedan.

3

"Hey, Anthony! Where have you been?" the manager yelled. "We haven't seen you in here in quite some time!"

"I know. Well, you know I'm at the university now. I'm only here now because of spring break. I have a whole week and then it's back to work! How are you guys doin'?" Anthony inquired. He used to work there, too, before he quit to enroll at the university two years ago.

"We're all great. Hey---what can we help ya with?" the young student at the counter asked.

"Well----I'll have a hamburger with fries and a chocolate milkshake," Anthony responded. He always ordered the same menu items every time he came in. Old habits are hard to break.

"What else?" the young man asked.

"Oh, yes, who was *that* girl who was just in here?" Anthony asked asking like he was joking, but he really wasn't. He was dead serious.

"That's Julie Johnson," the worker answered. "She is sooooo nice. Really. Plus beautiful! Why, are ya interested?" *Like who wouldn't be??*

"Why wouldn't I be interested? I'm not *blind*, you know!" Anthony joked. Anthony had a great personality and he was a great manager when he worked there before going to college. He got along with all of the other workers; they respected him. He had great rapport with the people who came into the Dairy Queen and not just the high schoolers. Their parents and their grandparents loved him, too!

4

As Julie drove home, she couldn't stop thinking about the handsome man she had just seen. He was so nice! His dark, brown hair was not too short and not too long. It was just perfect, actually. His eyes were a deep blue and had a message inside, but she couldn't figure out what it was. He dressed very neatly----a baby blue sweater over a white button down-collar shirt and cream-colored slacks. *How handsome! Maybe I should just keep my mind on my driving! And what a personality! He was the perfect gentleman.*

"How'd it go?" Julie's mother asked as she heard her enter the back door. "Did you get a lot of work done or did you get a lot of laughing done?" Gloria knew what those particular eight girls were like when they all got together.

"It was great. We really did get a lot of work done. Everyone seemed to pick up a job so we'll see how the party all comes together. I think it'll really be a lot of fun. It was great. Food was great, too." Julie answered as she walked to her room. "Has Dad gotten in yet?"

"No, Hun. He had a late meeting tonight, too."

"OK. I'm gonna turn in early tonight, Mom. Good night. Tell Dad 'Good night' for me." Julie said.

Julie wasn't really that tired, but she wanted to go to her room, so she could rethink the incident that occurred at the Dairy Queen. Not a replay of the committee meeting----but a replay of that handsome man opening the door for her and that spark of electricity that seemed to go from his eyes to hers.

Was I just imagining that? She asked herself. *OK— let me replay that in my mind. I was walking toward the door. He opened the door before I got there. I walked in. I thanked him. Our eyes met. There was definitely something there. Then I left. I don't remember anything else after that.*

Julie replayed the scene over and over in her mind, until she finally fell asleep.

Anthony thought about Julie also as he drove home.
At least he knew her name. Julie didn't know
Anthony's name. *She is such a pretty girl.* He
thought. *And she seems so nice. Obviously, she is
because that's what the guys there said. I know I
have a busy week, and I promised to do so many
things with my parents, but surely there is time to
track her down.*

He arrived at his parents' house and started
unloading the groceries he had picked up on his
way home. He wanted to do everything he could to
help his mother, since she always did so much for
him. She heard him unloading groceries in the
kitchen.

"Anthony! So glad you are here! Oh, you are so
sweet. Thank you for picking up the groceries. I
know you are probably tired from your trip," his
mother said knowing that it was a twelve-hour drive
from the university. "Did you have something to
eat?"

"Yes, I had to go to my old haunt—the Dairy
Queen. I just grabbed something, so you wouldn't
have to bother with fixin' anything," Anthony said
as he hugged his mother affectionately. He was
always so considerate.

Anthony's father entered the kitchen and playfully
put a neck hold around Anthony's neck. "How's it

goin' ol' college guy?" he joked. He was so proud of Anthony. Anthony was making excellent grades just like he did in high school and his father was particularly proud of the fact that Anthony was going to follow in his footsteps. His father was a financial advisor/stock broker and Anthony was studying to go into the same field.

"Would you guys quit fooling around?" his mother said. "You're not thirteen anymore. I don't want either of you getting hurt. I don't want to play nurse."

Both parents were so happy that they had a whole week to be with Anthony. When he is away at the university, they never get to see him. Since he is so busy from morning to night, they don't even get to talk to him very often. They really look forward to spring break, summer, Thanksgiving and Christmas.

They made plans for the family to visit with Anthony's uncle---his maternal uncle who lived about three hours away. It wouldn't be a big trip, but it would take up one complete day of spring break. It was important, though. Anthony's uncle was elderly, and the family didn't know how much more time they would have with him. One thing Anthony's parents instilled in him was the importance of family. It was a good attribute for them to have promoted. They also instilled honesty, integrity, faith, loyalty, and service to others.

Chapter 3
Hoping for a Meeting

While Anthony was with his parents on their trip, Julie thought about the incident at the Dairy Queen. She even tried to convince herself that nothing would ever come out of it.

You know, he is probably a college guy who just happens to be here at this time. He probably has a steady girlfriend there because how could he NOT have a steady girlfriend! He may not have a steady girlfriend which would then mean that he has SEVERAL girlfriends. He's probably covered up with girls. Why would he possibly be interested in me? It doesn't make sense. I have another year of high school! He probably thinks I'm in eighth grade or something.

The following day after school, even though she tried hard to talk herself out of the turmoil her mind was engaging in, she kept going back to the fact that she wanted to see him just one more time! *OK— that does it. I'm going back down to the Dairy Queen. He was there once---maybe he'll be there again. But, I know I've never seen him there before so he must be a college guy here for a college break.*

Julie jumped in the car and drove to the Dairy Queen. After parking her car, she nonchalantly walked through the door and took a seat in a booth near the front. Glancing around, she didn't see

Anthony, but if she sat near the front, she could see if he drove up.

Julie ordered a strawberry smoothie, sat down, and opened her notebook to make it look like she was going to work on something. She really wasn't. She glanced up at the door a million times. No handsome gentleman. *I don't even know his name.*

Julie waited about two hours before she gave up and walked toward the door. "Bye, guys!" she yelled cheerfully, or at least she tried to act cheerfully, as she left.

2

Not thirty minutes had gone by when Anthony arrived at the Dairy Queen. He had the same idea. *Just maybe. Just maybe she will show up*. He rationalized it this way: *If I don't go, I won't see her for sure. If I go, there is at least a chance that I will see her.*

"You just missed her, Anthony! She was here for almost two hours!" the young workers couldn't wait to tell him.

"Are you kidding? Was she with anyone? Why was she here for two hours? Anthony couldn't get the questions out fast enough.

"No---not kidding. She was by herself---sat right over there by herself. I think she was working on something, because she had a notebook and wrote things down in it every so often," the manager said entering in on the conversation. At least four workers had their eyes on Anthony.

I can't believe it! If I could have just gotten here a little earlier, I would have seen her again. Anthony mulled over in his head.

"Why don't you call her, Anthony?" the manager said. He thought that was the most logical thing to do. After all, everyone could tell Anthony was really smitten with Julie.

"Oh, I don't want to scare her away. I'm sure a beautiful girl like she is already in a relationship with Mr. Hotshot Football Quarterback. Well, I'll think about it." Anthony said as he headed for the door.

"Don't you want to order something?" the manager asked.

"Nah, I really need to be going." Anthony said as he walked out the door.

I bet he wouldn't really need to be goin' if she had been here, they thought.

OK, this is a little ridiculous. I can't believe I'm acting this way. Did I really drive down to the Dairy Queen to try to find her? Really? Mr. University Man? You need to get a grip. Anthony reprimanded himself.

It didn't really matter how much Anthony reprimanded himself. The following day, feeling that his spring break was slipping away, he ran errands with his mother, went to see his father at the office, and then rearranged his trip back home to conveniently pass by the Dairy Queen.

He made sure it was approximately the same time he knew she had been there the day before. Glancing at the cars, Anthony did not see a black Ford. *Well, she's not here now, but maybe she will come. Hopefully she will come. I'll pray that she comes.*

Anthony parked his car, walked through the door and greeted everyone at the counter.

"Well, well, well----you're back," the workers teased. "I bet you order something this time!"

"You are a bunch of smart alecks. But, yes, I am rather hungry. I've been running errands all day long, and you know how that can be," Anthony tried to say convincingly. They knew better. He may actually be hungry, but the real reason he was there was to see if Julie might happen to come in.

He paid for his order and then sat in the same booth Julie sat in a day earlier. Coincidence. Just as he started eating his hamburger, a black Ford pulled into the parking lot.

Anthony almost started hyperventilating. *Did I see that correctly? Is Julie really driving into the parking lot? Is anyone with her? What am I going to do? I can't let her get away this time. OK--- calm down.*

If Julie had known what car Anthony was driving, she probably would have started hyperventilating too! But, she didn't know what car he drove or even what his name was. She was just going to try one more time. No amount of trying to talk her out of the situation worked on her, either. She had to go.

Julie parked her car, walked up to the door, and sure enough, Anthony was there once again, opening the door for her. She couldn't believe it. *Oh my gosh! Oh my gosh!* That's all she could say to herself.

"Julie, come in. Get in out of that wind. It's turning kind of cold." Anthony said calmly as if he talked to her every day.

Julie? How does he know my name? she thought in a split second.

"Why, thank you very much. I remember you from before," the biggest smile on her face came naturally. "Now, how is it you know my name and I don't know yours?"

"I guess you are just special. Everyone seems to know your name. Everyone. Let me introduce myself to you," Anthony said graciously as he led her to the front counter. "But first, what would you like to order? Will you join me? I've just started eating."

Julie was so blown away with the encounter that she couldn't even remember what she usually ordered. She certainly wasn't hungry at that point.

"Oh, I really just want a strawberry smoothie," she said rather nervously. "And I'd love to join you, if you don't mind."

Don't mind? Don't mind? Anthony thought to himself. *Are you kidding?*

"Well, actually I do mind, but I'm very good to people who are sort of down and out, you know--- people who don't have anything going for them. I always feel sorry for that type, so I try to help them out. Since I know no one else would want *you* to sit with *him*, I'm going to offer my assistance," Anthony said as he tried to look serious---but burst out laughing.

He didn't know whom he was dealing with. Quick as a wink, Julie twirled on her heels and headed for the door. She was so quick, Anthony had to grab her arm to keep her from leaving. She tried to act seriously, too, but she couldn't contain her laughter after the first ten seconds.

"Woah! Are you a track star or something?" he said wanting to hold onto her arm longer but thinking it wasn't appropriate. *This is sooo good. She is sooo special.*

"Well, actually I am. I mean, I'm not a STAR, but I've been known to win a few races from time to time. Could ya tell?" she replied with a twinkle in her eye.

"Let's just say this. I wouldn't want to be in any race with you---anytime---anywhere---for anything."

"OK, be sure to remember that. Now, weren't you going to introduce yourself to me? Now, be truthful. You don't have a criminal record do you?" Julie was starting to feel a little more comfortable.

"Miss Johnson, I am Anthony Adkins. Nice meeting you." He shook her hand with meaning. "I do NOT have a criminal record, because the two murder convictions and three bank robberies were magically expunged from my record. It always helps to know people in high places. Don't worry, I won't rob or kill you. I promise."

Julie knew this was going to be an interesting evening. They sat and talked for three hours, before they finally decided that they had family waiting for them at home, and they should really get back. Anthony's mother and father were probably waiting for him to come in, so they could plan for the rest of the week. Julie's parents didn't really know where she was, but they really never worried. It's just that they would be wondering.

4

Julie was on top of the world. She finally met the handsome gentleman, and he turned out to have the greatest personality ever. He was perfect---perfect in every way. Then she started worrying. He was too perfect. *Why would he be interested in me?*

Anthony floated home. His car tires didn't even touch the road. He had finally met the beautiful girl and then he finds out she is cleaver and witty. She was perfect. Perfect in every way. *But why would she be interested in me? And I'll be going back to the university in a few days, so I guess that will be the end of it. Would it have been better if I hadn't met her at all?*

He answered his own question. *No, it's not better to have never met her. It's better to have met her and lost her than to never have met her at all. OK, then. But don't be sad when you have to leave. Just enjoy every minute that you can spend with her and be thankful. Be thankful.*

Anthony pulled out the white napkin that he had written her phone number on and committed the number to memory. He would be calling her the next morning for sure.

Chapter 4
The Beginning of the Beginning

Julie knew she gave Anthony her phone number last night but that was last night when they were having so much fun talking and being funny. *Maybe he has had time think about it. He may have a girlfriend back at the university so, although he got my phone number, he may never really call.*

She told herself not to expect anything. But, she couldn't help thinking about how much fun they were both having.

"Rrring. Rrring. Rrring" the phone sounded after Julie and her parents had just finished eating breakfast. She grabbed the phone.

"Julie?" Anthony asked on the other end of the line.

"Yes? Anthony?" Julie said.

"No, 'mam. I'm Mr. Gotcha calling from the law enforcement office in Lubbock County. We are investigating a sleazy criminal who is wanted for murder and robbery. We understand you met with him last night at the local Dairy Queen? We have some questions for you," Anthony said trying to disguise his voice but doing a pretty poor job.

"Happy to help you! You are absolutely correct. He is sleazy, and he admitted to me that he killed those people and he robbed those banks. I'll wear a wire! Let's do it!" Julie joked but tried to act seriously. The next three minutes was a solid stream of laughter on both ends of the telephone line.

When it finally ended, Anthony said, "I knew you'd sell me out. Boy, that is pathetic. And I had every intention of having you join up with me. Of course, you'd get your cut of the bank money---1%."

"So generous!" she replied. "I risk my life---risk getting shot---for 1% take? Please! Do you think I'm a fool?"

"Well, I won't answer that question, but I do have a question for you," Anthony said.

"What is it?" she answered.

"Would you go to dinner with me tonight?" this time he really was serious.

Julie answered quickly, "Do you mind if I wait to see if anybody else asks me? I mean, I don't want to keep you hanging on, but if anybody else calls, I might just have to take them up on their invitation. I usually get several calls per day."

This is the first time that Anthony thought someone else was beating him at his game. Julie was fast. She could think on her feet so quickly.

"Sure---you can do that. After all, I've already asked five girls to dinner, but their calendars were booked with meetings and events. So, you were kind of low on the list, anyway. Feel free to wait because if it doesn't work out, I really don't care."

This bantering couldn't last forever.

"OK, OK. I give up. Do you see me waving the white flag? Can you see it over the phone?" Julie asked.

"Whew!" he said. "I was running out of material. How about I pick you up tonight at 6:30?"

"That'll be perfect. I'll see you then." Julie answered.

2

Julie walked on clouds for the rest of the day. All she could think of was Anthony. She attended her classes as usual, but she really didn't listen to anything going on. *What am I going to wear? How should I wear my hair? I wonder where we will be going?*

When she got home after school, she told her mother that she had a special date with a special gentleman named Anthony Adkins. "He's a college sophomore mom, but we had so much fun when we talked at the Dairy Queen. He is so funny and is so smart. Laughter is good."

"Well, I want you to have a good time. Of course, no one is as smart or as funny or as clever as you, my cutie. Well, I'm your mom---does that count?"
"Yes, Mom, it counts. I love you." Julie hugged her mom.

3

Anthony pulled up to Julie's house exactly three minutes before he told her he would be there. That's because he is never late to anything. Julie was looking out of her bedroom window when he got out of his car. He looked absolutely stunning.

Anthony was wearing a cream-colored sweater with black slacks. Not a single hair was out of place. Julie thought he was the most handsome man she had ever seen.

After his knock on the door, Julie's mother opened it just as Julie walked into the living room. What Julie hadn't seen as he walked up the sidewalk were the two peach-colored roses he held. He handed one to Julie's mother and one to Julie. *So sweet!* Julie thought.

"Mrs. Johnson, I'm Anthony Adkins and very pleased to meet you. Thank you for allowing me to enjoy your daughter's company tonight."

"Anthony, you must be quite special. Take care of my daughter and y'all have a great time," she answered.

Anthony and Julie walked to the car; he opened the door and helped her into the car. Such a gentleman.

"What do you think about going to Remington's tonight? It is such a nice steak house, but you can get anything there. There are really nice salads and all kinds of pasta dishes," Anthony said. "However, they may *not* have strawberry smoothies." They chuckled together.

"I think that would be great, Anthony. If you like it, I'm sure I'll like it." Julie just couldn't believe she was going to be with him for dinner and conversation. *Life is perfect*, she thought.

4

Julie and Anthony were led to their booth near the back of the restaurant. The lights were low and the background music was soft enough to talk easily. It seemed like the perfect atmosphere to get to know someone.

"Julie, tell me about your earliest memory," Anthony said. "How far back in your childhood can you actually remember?"

"I don't know how old I was, but I remember several things. Once, my family and I were at the park in our little hometown. I don't know if it was a July 4th picnic or not but it was an event such as that. I remember someone was carrying me around. It wasn't my mother or father but a teenaged girl.

There was some kind of little activity where prizes were given. I remember seeing a young girl, maybe 6 or 7, winning a small plastic purse. It would have been a purse for a small doll of some kind. Well, I wanted that purse. I remember crying and crying. The girl who held me tried to calm me down but nothing would work. Finally, either the girl who had won the purse or someone else, a small girl, came up to me to give me the purse. I instantly quit crying. I'm a little embarrassed by the memory. Was I spoiled or what! I guess I was only two or three years old at the time! I wish I knew exactly how old I was."

Anthony listened to the whole story with a smile on his face. "There was another time---I don't know if this was before or after the purse incident, but my brother and I were in our backyard, right out the back door under a tree. My brother dug a small hole as deeply as he could. Actually, it was probably only about twelve to fifteen inches deep at the most. Anyway, he dug the hole with a kitchen spoon. When it looked pretty deep, he put his ear to the hole. He told me he was listening for the devil.

He let me put my ear to the hole. I couldn't hear a thing, but I believed him when he said he could hear the devil. Evidently, my grandmother, who lived next door saw the whole thing through her window. She probably heard the conversation, too, because later I heard her tell my mother something about it."

Anthony had to laugh at this one. "Well," he said, "You were at least digging in the right direction!"

"I can also remember, about that same time, my father teaching my brother how to play the harmonica----although we called it a French harp in those days. My brother sat on the back steps with my dad sitting beside him. I was sitting there, too, so I watched intently. My father used a hand signal to show my brother when to breathe in and when to blow out. At first, my father moved the harmonica in front of my brother's mouth---making sure to hit the right notes for the song. My brother blew out and breathed in according to my father's hand signal. I was mesmerized. I think the song was 'You Are My Sunshine' although I also remember 'Under the Double Eagle.' I can recall that lesson vividly--- as if it were yesterday. Today my brother can play the harmonica beautifully. I can't play a lick-----but I'm good at sitting and watching. Ha."

Julie seemed to be enjoying herself---- reminiscing about her childhood brought nice memories and Brandon really enjoyed hearing her stories.

"Oh, my gosh!" Julie said opening her eyes as widely as she could. "I have another memory that is unbelievable! It really happened, though."

Anthony couldn't wait to hear her story.

"Remember I told you about my family being at the park?" Julie said.

"Is this the same park?" Anthony interrupted.

"Actually, yes, it was. It was the only park in town so it had to be!" she answered. "Well, I don't know if it was the same summer or not, but I have another really vivid memory. Again, I was very, very young. My parents parked their new car on the side of the park where everyone was congregating. Sometime during the picnic, my brother led me over to the car. Of course, the doors were unlocked---you even left your house unlocked in those days! He sat behind the wheel and I climbed up into the front passenger seat. I watched while he pushed in the cigarette lighter. After a few seconds, the lighter popped out---a signal that it was ready and hot enough to light the end of a cigarette. Of course, I watched every move my brother made- --I always did. He took the cigarette lighter out of the holder in the dashboard and started burning holes into the vinyl seat that was between where we were sitting. One after another, he pushed the cigarette lighter onto the seat, burning the vinyl and leaving perfect circles burned into the seat. I remember seeing four or five circles. He seemed to think it was fun. I remember thinking that it probably wasn't a good thing. That is where the memory ends. I don't remember leaving the car or if someone came to find us. I don't remember any reaction once my dad saw the seat. I don't recall anything. Oh, my gosh! I wonder what my dad did when he saw that!"

"It's a good thing you didn't take after your brother!" Anthony said with a laugh. "And you say he is really a good guy now?"

"Model citizen," Julie replied with a laugh. "Those are my earliest memories. I have many more, but I was older, of course. It's funny to think back on those things."

"Tell me more," Anthony said, partly because he loved to hear Julie tell stories and partly because he didn't want the day to end. If she kept telling stories, maybe it would never end.

"I remember I used to get terrible earaches when I was a child. It was so windy where I grew up and, of course, I played outside all of the time. I was a real tomboy." Julie started to go on, but Anthony interrupted.

"You were a tomboy? You----with golden curls and flowers in your hair? A tomboy?" Anthony acted totally amazed at the thought.

"Yes—definitely. In fact, I was very proud of the fact that I didn't wear a dress to school for two straight years. I had to wear a dress to church, but I always wore pants to school. *That* was being a tomboy."

Anthony had a look of disbelief on his face. "Go on," he said.

"Well, back to the earaches. I remember getting terrible earaches *every* time I played out in the wind. I remember getting a horrible earache right at Christmas time. When I raised my head up off the pillow, a terrible, yellow liquid ran out of my ear onto the pillowcase. It also sounded like Niagra Falls was in my ear. My dad took me to Dr. Jaynes the next day. Dr. Jaynes looked into my right ear with his instrument and then told my father to look also. "See the hole in her eardrum? She'll need some penicillin to fix this," the doctor said. He gave me a shot (I abhorred needles in those days) and I had to go back for two additional shots. After my eardrum healed, I never had another earache---- not for the rest of my life. That penicillin really worked!"

Julie leaned over and hugged Anthony gently as if to thank him for listening to her. Then, she abruptly straightened up and said," Oh no----- another memory----not good. Ya want to hear it?"

"Of course," Anthony said, "Are you kidding! Tell me more."

"Well, when I was very young---must have been only three or four years old---my brother and I were in my grandmother's kitchen. All of the adults were sitting in the living room, talking and laughing. As usual, I followed my brother and watched every move he made out of total curiosity.

Of course, I did! He was always doing something! Remember the cigarette lighter? Well, anyway, he had turned the gas burner on the stove on and I could barely see the flame from where I stood. I must have been pretty small because I had to look up to see the burners. My brother had a fork in his hand, and he put the fork in the flame to make it really hot. I also remember he had to reach up to put the fork in the flame, so he must have been pretty little, also. I watched in total amazement as he carefully heated the fork. I had never seen anyone holding an eating fork in a flame of fire before! Then in one swift movement, he grabbed my little, skinny arm and pressed the fork onto the skin right at the bend of my elbow. In other words, he branded me. I remember letting out a blood- curdling scream and that is where the memory ends. Can you imagine what happened next? I'm sure someone ran to my side only to find a fresh brand of a fork on my arm. The four prongs of the fork remained on my arm and can even be seen today--- see? Of course, they are really faded now and have spread but can you see?"

Anthony leaned over and took her left arm in his hands to get a closer look. Sure enough, Anthony could make out the scar faintly.

"This is unbelievable!" Anthony said halfway laughing but halfway feeling very sorry for Julie. "You poor little thing. Is that why you're so tough today?" Anthony said pulling her close to him. "Well, you don't have to be tough anymore. I'll protect you and keep these things from happening to you." He hugged her gently.

"OK, since I've gotten pity from you on that one, let me tell you what else he used to do to me."

"Uh-oh---can I take it?" Anthony asked looking out of the corner of his eye.

"Sure," Julie continued." I always wanted to tag along with my brother---I told you that. He usually didn't want me tagging along so he would take off my shoes and would leave me standing in the middle of a sticker patch. I remember standing there crying and not moving one inch. He had me believe that if I moved one step, I'd step right into a bunch of stickers. Of course, I probably could have inched my way out, but I never remember trying. I guess I cried until someone came to my rescue! I just remember standing there crying. What a baby I was!"

"Is that why you became a tomboy?" Anthony asked. "I think all of that toughened you up! So, what happened-----you don't seem like a tomboy now---not at all!"

"Oh, I don't know. I just loved running and jumping and doing those tomboy things. I never played with baby dolls, either. Mom said that when I was very young, she bought me a baby doll thinking that's what all little girls love. To her disappointment, I didn't pay any attention at all to the beautiful baby doll. Mom said I put the doll down and then started playing with the trucks my brother got. You know what I loved and was interested in the most?" Julie said with eyebrows lifted.

"I can't imagine. You tell me," Anthony said.

"I loved playing with horses---you know, the toy type. I'd imagine they were real. I was in heaven if I had a toy horse to play with. Once my mother bought me a rather large, white, toy horse. I remember holding it against the window sill of the car so everyone could see it. I was so proud of that horse. I think it was about nine inches tall so that was huge compared to the others I had."

"So, you really loved horses?" Anthony asked.

"Oh, yes! And I always wanted a real one. A friend of mine, Debbie, had several *real* horses. She lived on the edge of town. I always thought she was so lucky to have real horses. But she was a really good rider. She entered barrel racing competitions at the local rodeos---and she won! I could never do that, but I really admired her for her talent. I felt lucky just to get to ride with her."

"Would you like to have a real horse now?" Anthony asked.

"Oh, yes! But, to be realistic, I can't take care of a horse while I'm still in school. Maybe I could get one someday. I think they're such beautiful animals.

I watched Roy Rogers and Dale Evans on television as a child and their horses were magnificent! Trigger and Buttermilk, I believe."

They talked and talked and then finally ordered. Dinner was both delicious and beautiful. The service was perfect. They talked about the high school and the university and their favorite teachers and professors. They talked about sports and their favorite teams. They talked about their favorite movies and songs. Finally, after about two hours into the conversation, Anthony asked, "Julie---I can't believe you agreed to go out with me. I was afraid you were involved in another relationship with some great guy."

"No, no, I'm not. I have a lot of great guy friends but no one I'm really interested in. I haven't been interested in dating. I've been pretty busy, also," Julie answered hoping she was saying the right thing. "What about you?"

"I'm so busy at the university, that I really don't have time to date anyone. Like you, I have some really good friends, but no, no one special," he answered sincerely. That was music to Julie's ears.

"I know you will be going back to the university sometime Sunday for classes on Monday. Thank you for letting me have so much fun while you've been here. I think I've laughed more in the last few days than I have in the last year!" Julie meant it.

Feeling that they were nearing the end of the evening, Julie pulled a Lincoln-head penny out of her purse. She lay it on the tablecloth near Anthony's drinking glass.

"What is that?" he asked as he looked at the penny. "I don't think that is quite enough for the tip."

"Well, it's just a little message. When you find a penny that is lying heads up, it means I'm thinking about you. Remember that."

"OK! I will! Are you ready to go now? I think I better get you home before your parents send out a search party," Anthony said as he helped Julie up from her chair. He placed his arm around her waist softly as they walked to the front door. Julie felt so safe and loved in his presence.

It was almost sad as they drove to her house. They both knew the evening was ending. The lights were on in the living room which meant her parents were reading and talking about the events of the day, so Anthony welcomed the invitation to join them for a few minutes.

Julie asked to be excused once Anthony joined her parents. He thought she was making a quick trip to the restroom, perhaps. She had a different idea.

Walking through the house, she grabbed a penny out of her purse, quietly slipped through the back door and ran around to the front of the house.

Getting to Anthony's car, she lifted up the windshield wiper on the driver's side and placed the penny underneath it so that he would see a Lincoln head penny right in front of his eyes----heads up.

After just a couple of minutes, Julie joined Anthony and her parents in the living room. "We had the greatest time!" she exclaimed.

"Yes, we've already heard," Mrs. Johnson answered. Julie smiled at Anthony. They talked for a few more minutes about the university Anthony attended and then it was time to leave.

"I'll be going now. Thank you all again," he said as he walked with Julie toward the front door. "I'll call you tomorrow, if that is OK with you, Julie."

Julie smiled as Anthony turned and walked down the sidewalk to his car. She closed the door behind him. Smiling, she walked to her room. *He should just about be reaching his car. He'll get in, look up, he'll be puzzled at why his windshield wiper is up. Then he'll see the penny.*

Since it was dark outside, Julie couldn't look out her window and see the car clearly. Then she saw Anthony open the car door, because the light came on, and she faintly saw him move the wiper back into place. *He put something in his pocket. It's the penny! I know he put the penny in his pocket! Mission accomplished.* She couldn't be happier. *OK, he should remember what the penny means.*

She went to sleep thinking about the wonderful evening they had together. It couldn't have been better. *What a fantastic person Anthony is!*

As Anthony drove home, he couldn't quit thinking about Julie. *And the penny? How creative is that? How did she do that? I guess when she excused herself? But she was only gone a few seconds! How did she do it?*

Chapter 5
End of Spring Break

"Son," Anthony's dad said at breakfast the next morning. "I really need you to catch a flight to Denver this weekend to sit in on a meeting for me. I just can't go because of everything else going on, but you'd be the perfect person to fill in."

Normally, Anthony would have loved the opportunity to fly to Denver, but now? Now when he was so interested in a relationship with Julie? They only had the weekend left and this would certainly cut into their time together.

"What day is the meeting, Dad?" Anthony asked trying to sound interested.

"Well, you could fly down Saturday evening and catch a fight back Sunday evening. I know that would mean you'd drive back to the university on Monday, and you'd have to miss a day of school," he answered. "Can you do that?"

Anthony was relieved that he would only miss one day with Julie. And he certainly didn't mind missing classes on Monday. Monday was a light day for him, and he wasn't going to have any tests. His project for one class was well on its way, so Monday classes would be fine to miss.

Anthony met Julie for lunch on Saturday. They joked and kidded like they always did when they were together, but then Anthony had to get serious.

"Julie, my father needs me to attend a meeting for him in Denver tomorrow. Luckily, I can fly up this evening late, stay one night, and catch a flight back later tomorrow afternoon. I hope I can see you when I get back for dinner or something. I'll just drive back to the university on Monday."

"Sure," Julie answered trying to sound very serious. "I'd love to see you----well, that is if my first and second choice of dates aren't available. OK— forget that---what were you going to say?"

"I'm normally happy to fill in for my father. I've done it a couple of times. Especially in Denver. The conference is at the Colorado Mountain Lodge and Resort and the accommodations are the greatest! But, someone has come into my life and my priorities have changed," he said.

When Anthony mentioned where he would be staying, Julie made a mental note. She had a plan up her sleeve.

"Well, I think my priorities have changed, too. I am so happy when I am with you. I think it is great that you are helping out your dad. I'll miss you tremendously, but I will manage. Let's have fun today!" Julie tried to sound happy, but she was really quite sad.

Anthony and Julie had a great time on Saturday, talking and laughing. They had lunch together, then went for a walk in the park around the lake. They caught a movie in the afternoon and then had a quick bite to eat before he left for the airport.

2

Arriving at the lodge, Anthony checked into his room around 10:00 pm and then gathered what he needed for the meeting. He looked forward to getting to bed---to think about the wonderful time he had with Julie before heading for the airport. He would have liked to have stayed with her, but he knew his father needed him and he was willing to help out.

Meanwhile, Julie was putting her plan into action. She called the lodge in Denver.

"Hello, Colorado Mountain Lodge and Resort, may I help you?" the attendant answered.

"I really hope you can. I have a friend who will be checking into your lodge later today. This is kind of a personal joke. Is there any way that you or someone there could tape several pennies to a sheet of paper heads up? I know this sounds really strange. but it will really turn out great. I'll pay you for your trouble," Julie pleaded into the phone.

"Oh, no. No. No trouble. We aim to please. I'm happy to do it myself. Now, what did you say to do exactly?" he inquired.

"You could just get a sheet of your stationery, tape several pennies---or one or two---onto the page heads up----*has* to be heads up. Then fold the paper, place in the envelope and slide under his door late tonight or early in the morning. His name is Anthony Adkins."

"Consider it done, m'am," he answered. Julie was pleased. *He's gonna love this*, she thought.

3

Anthony jumped out of bed the next morning to get ready for his meeting when he heard something sliding under his door. Looking toward the door, he noticed a white envelope on the carpet.

Probably my bill since I'm only here one night, he thought to himself. He walked toward the door, picked up the envelope and opened it. Unfolding the paper, he saw four pennies taped to the paper--- heads up.

> *I'm thinking of you.*
> *I'm thinking of you.*
> *I'm thinking of you.*
> *I'm thinking of you.*

Julie, you are so special. I can't believe you did this.

Anthony couldn't wait to get back home. He was later glad that he took notes to tell his dad, because he had trouble listening to the speakers. His mind was on Julie the whole time. *Pennies!*

4

Anthony's plane landed at 6:37 pm Sunday evening. He could be home by 7:15 and could pick Julie up at 7:45. He would call her from the airport.

He didn't realize just how sad the evening was going to be. When they realized that he would be going back to school the next day, and she wouldn't even be able to see him until the end of the semester, it was hard to take. Letters would be fine and the best way to communicate because trying to use the phone in the dorm was so inconvenient, not to mention those long-distance charges that stack up faster than one can imagine. They decided to do their best to be the best students they could be, stay focused on school (and sports for Julie), and then look forward to the summer vacation.

They had a lovely dinner, but soon the evening was coming to an end. When Julie excused herself to go to the ladies' room, it was Anthony's chance. He took a very shiny penny from his pocket and slid it under the napkin she had just placed on the table.

When Julie returned and picked up the napkin, she saw the penny. It was a complete surprise. She was

the one always thinking of planting pennies! Now
he did it, too!

"I'm thinking of you," she said as she picked up the
penny.

"Truer words were never spoken," he said as he
leaned over to kiss her on the cheek.

"Hey, Anthony," Julie said cheerfully to keep things
from turning sad. "I saw a sweatshirt that said this:

> *You know that little thing inside your*
> *head that keeps you from saying things*
> *you shouldn't? Yeah, I don't have*
> *one of those.*

Anthony loved it. He laughed *so* hard.

Then Julie had another one:

> *I meant to behave but there were just too*
> *many other options.*

Her mission was accomplished. She wanted to end
the evening with laughter.

It was the perfect ending to a beautiful evening.

Chapter 6
Reunion for the Summer

The time between spring break and the end of the semester seemed like an eternity for both of them. Julie was always very busy with her schoolwork and her sports and various clubs and organizations. The party that Julie and her committee worked on was coming together and was scheduled for the last week of school. They felt they had just the right location, just the right caterer, just the right entertainment, and just the right music. That committee of eight did a great job.

Anthony was equally busy with his classes and an internship that he had to complete. They thought of each other often but were thankful their lives were so full.

Finally, the semester ended at the university. Anthony piled everything he owned in his car and headed home. He had plenty of time to think about her on the drive home. In fact, he thought about her the entire way home. *Boy, she really has a hold on me!* he thought. *But I like it.*

Julie knew he was going to be driving home very soon but didn't really know when that was going to be. He had to take his final exams and close out his dorm room.

Anthony started out early enough so that he could get to Julie's high school before she got out for the day. He wanted to surprise her. He pulled into the parking lot about fifteen minutes before the last bell. He left a note on her windshield:

Julie, I just got in and wanted to meet
you at the Dairy Queen to relive old times
if you can meet me there. If you aren't there in
thirty minutes I'll know that you a) have forgotten
about me and don't know who I am, b) would rather
drive off a cliff or c) fell in love with Mr. High
School Quarterback so won't give me the time of
day.

Anthony then drove to the Dairy Queen to wait for her. He couldn't wait to see her. He was only there a few minutes when her car pulled into the parking lot. *Whew! I didn't scare her off.*

He jumped up to open the door for her exactly how he had done on the other two occasions. When their eyes met, there was the same electricity that had been there before. No, actually, it was much stronger. They sat in the booth at the back and talked for hours. Mainly, they talked about all of the things they wanted to do over the summer. They would be doing as many things together as possible. They talked about going to the beach, water skiing in the nearby lake, fishing in Anthony's favorite spot, going on picnics, going to movies and plays, and just about everything else they could think to do.

Then Julie brought up more of her sweatshirt sayings:

Exercise? I thought you said extra fries!

Once is a while, someone amazing comes along. Here I am!

Anthony laughed again but told her he actually agreed with the second one. *You are amazing, Julie!*

Julie still had about two weeks of school left. Anthony helped his parents with everything they needed during the day and then he got to spend time with Julie in the evening.

It didn't take long for everyone to notice that Anthony and Julie were together every minute they could be. They appeared to be the perfect couple. Julie's parents were totally impressed with Anthony and Anthony's parents were totally impressed with Julie, or at least his mother was. His dad remained silent. The only reason his father remained silent was that he always thought that Anthony needed to have the best connections in order to get ahead in his field. He could work his way up the hard way, or he could marry into the right family and climb the ladder much faster. Mr. Adkins had just the person in mind for Anthony.

2

Then summer came to a close. Julie had to go back to school a week before Anthony had to leave for the university. It was the hardest thing she ever had to do. They made it from spring break to the end of the school year, but it really wasn't that long. Now, they were faced with being apart for almost *three months*. Thanksgiving would be the first time for them to spend time together, again.

The send-off was terrible. Anthony loaded up his car then drove to Julie's house to say "good-bye." She couldn't keep from crying no matter how hard she tried to be strong. At first, she tried to strategically hide the tears, but at the end, she couldn't. This reaction was hard for Anthony to take. His heart was breaking.

It was so difficult for Julie because of things that went through her head. *I love Anthony. I love him more than anything in the world. He's going to be gone for so long. Am I going to lose him? I's not good that we are going to be apart.*

Basically, Anthony's feelings were the same. She was just too pretty, too sweet, too clever, too friendly, too intelligent, too humorous, too…..too…..everything.

Julie's father saw that Julie was the busiest girl at school. She played basketball, played volleyball, played tennis, and ran track. In addition, she was a majorette for the marching band. Her father's only concern was that Julie never cooked or baked anything. *Nothing!* He talked to one of his fellow colleagues one day and mentioned to him that Julie seemed to have many talents, but he worried about the poor guy she married because she didn't know how to cook. "She can't even boil water!" he told his friend, Brandon.

Unfortunately, Brandon was the father of Julie's best friend, Debbie. Once when Julie was at Debbie's house, Brandon told the story to the girls. "Yep, your dad is worried about the poor guy you marry someday. He's says you can't even boil water." Everyone laughed, and Debbie certainly knew that Julie never cooked, but she didn't do any cooking either!! Maybe her dad said that to get the message to both girls!

Julie never said a word about her father's concern. She just took the cookbook out one day, picked the item that she thought would be the most challenging to make, then set out to prove him wrong. After all, didn't he tell her that she could do *anything* if she put her mind to it?

Julie decided to make homemade yeast rolls. Isn't that pretty difficult? But she didn't want to make just plain old rolls. *Why not make homemade crescent rolls! Cut the dough into triangles and then roll them up to form crescents. Brush with butter and gently curve the ends. Yes! That's what I'll do!* And she did. The rolls came out beautifully and they were delicious.

I don't know what the big deal is about cooking and baking. Julie thought to herself. *There's a cookbook for everything. If you can read a book, can't you make a recipe?* Years later when Julie really did get into cooking and baking, she realized that it isn't as easy as just reading a recipe. There is definitely an element of 'experience' that makes a big difference. But, for the most part, read the recipe.

Julie's father never said anything about her cooking or baking again.

Chapter 7
Unexpected Move

One day, Mr. Johnson was called into his supervisor's office when he arrived at work.

"Johnson," his supervisor said in a very friendly manner. "You have done such a great job here at the plant. We want you to take over the managerial position at the new plant in Connecticut. It'll be a giant promotion for you. What do you think?"

"I'm honored, Thom, but I thought I had to have a degree as a requirement. I know I can do the job, but I'm just wondering," he inquired.

"Normally, yes---but we are so happy with your work that we are waiving that requirement. We've all talked about it and everyone is in agreement. You've got the job if you want it," Thom explained.

Julie's father arrived home earlier than usual that Monday. He had just found out that his company wanted to transfer him to the main operation site in Connecticut and he wanted to discuss it with his wife.

"How will this affect Julie? She will have to leave the school she has been in from the start. You know she is Miss Bradfield High School! Her sports team members will die. She is one of the main players," her father said hesitantly in conversation to his wife.

"She could possibly stay here for her senior year. Aunt Gena would love to take her in. Actually, they adore each other. I'd hate not having her around us, but I would be willing to let her do whatever she chooses," replied his wife.

"If she did that, then she could move up here after she graduates. She'd be heading off to college shortly after that. I wonder what she and Anthony are planning. They are so close. She is crazy about his and he is crazy about her. Anthony would have one more year. I guess Julie could attend the same university if it came to that."

Julie's parents speculated what might happen, but there was no way of really knowing anything. There were so many variables! They were given one month to get everything ready for their move. The company bought their home from them, so that problem was alleviated. Since their furniture and larger items would be moved by the company, they just needed to pack up their personal items.

The biggest concern was Julie. Did she want to stay? Did she want to move with them? What was best? They wanted her to be happy. She would be making the decision. It was a lot to think about.

Then two weeks into the discussion, the answer became easier. Julie started feeling sick and nauseous in the mornings. At first, she thought it was the flu. It continued, so she went to the doctor. Julie learned that she was pregnant. *We were together only one time.* She was in total shock. She had never been with anyone else ever---and would never be---but Anthony was different. They both let down their guard.

Julie told her parents that she would be moving with them to Connecticut. She wanted to be with her mother during this time and also didn't want word getting back to Anthony. She thought moving pretty far away would keep her news from reaching Anthony.

"Julie, don't you think you should tell Anthony?" her mother asked sincerely.

"Mother, I can't. I just can't. I know you may think this is the best thing, but it would change everything. Anthony would feel that he had to quit school to take care of me. He has to get his degree without the distraction of a family. And, I don't want this to force him into a decision concerning me. He is so honorable, he would absolutely marry me and take care of me. But, I want his decision to marry me to be because that is truly what he wants, not what he feels he *should* do. Do you understand me, Mom? I'm so sorry for this. I really am."

"Julie, I respect your feelings. I just want what is best for you---always. Your dad and I love you more than life itself. We will get through this. We will take care of you. I know everything will work out," her mom said.

Knowing that Anthony knew nothing of the move to Connecticut, Julie decided to write a letter to him explaining. The letter mentioned nothing about the pregnancy:

Dear Anthony,

What a shock! My father was offered the promotion of a lifetime by the president of his company. My parents said that I could finish out my senior year by living with my Aunt Gena, but I just didn't want to spend the last year I may have with my parents away from them. My biggest concern is being farther away from you.

When you return for Thanksgiving, I won't be there. I won't be there for Christmas, either. Would you consider visiting me and my family in Connecticut for Thanksgiving or Christmas or both? I love you and can't stand the thought of being away from you that long. There's also the possibility of spending next summer with Aunt Gena before we both go to the university. Your last year will be my first year.

However, I may be expecting too much. I don't want to take you for granted. If you think this long-distance relationship can work out, please get back to me. If you don't want this, I will understand.

I thank God every day that we got to be together last summer. I have never been happier in my life. But the decision needs to be yours. I'll wait to hear.

I Will Always Love You...I Promise
Julie

2

Julie finished the letter but realized she did not have
Anthony's mailing address. He was moving into a
new apartment but he didn't have the address when
they talked last. She would need to ask his parents.
Then she accidentally ran into one of his best
friends at the pharmacy. Albert was one of his best
friends and had already heard all about Julie.

"Albert! How are you? What are you doing here?
Aren't you supposed to be at the university?" Julie
was puzzled.

"Yes, I'm still there. I see Anthony all the time.
I'm just here for a special project, but I'll be back to
school in a week. Do you need to get something to
Anthony?" he asked.

"Actually, I do. Would you please get this letter to
him? I don't have his new address. I could get it
from his parents, but if you are going back and you
see him, I'd rather know that it is being hand-
delivered. It's very important."

"Certainly, I'll certainly get it to him," Albert
answered with conviction.

Albert took the letter, slipped it into the side pocket
of his briefcase and continued running errands for

his project. Passing through one of the office buildings, Albert ran into Anthony's father in the foyer.

"Mr. Adkins! How nice to see you!" he said.

"Albert. I thought you were at the university. You didn't drop out, did ya?" he said jokingly. "Why, Anthony's mom and I are going to see him tomorrow. I have to fly up there for a meeting, so we're planning to have dinner with him."

"Oh, wow! I'm glad you mentioned that. I have a letter that Julie wrote to Anthony. I agreed to deliver it, but I won't be back for a week. Here, let me give this to you. Would you give it to him tomorrow?"

"Sure will. Thanks," Mr. Adkins said as Albert fished it out of his briefcase and handed it to him.

Mr. Adkins took the envelope. He stared at it for a few seconds and then put it in his inside coat pocket.

3

Mr. Johnson thought about the letter. He didn't want his son to be involved with Julie. He had noticed how close they were getting over the summer and was glad when Anthony had to return to the university. He didn't want anything getting in the way of Anthony's graduating. Also, he didn't think that Julie was from the type of family that could bolster his profession. Julie's family members were hard-working people, but they didn't have the connections that some other people had. He had a conversation with his wife before they left on the trip and certainly before having dinner with Anthony.

"Gloria, I don't think Julie is the right person for Anthony. She seems so sweet and is certainly beautiful, but that's about all. She just doesn't have the connections that someone like Marilyn Kennedy has. Marilyn's family is wealthy, and they're surrounded by wealthy people all the time. If Anthony is going to be a financial planner/stock broker, he'll need all the connections he can get," he said confidently.

"Since when should a marriage be based on financial gain alone?" she asked with some concern. "You did well establishing your clientele, and I wasn't one of those wealthy debutantes," she argued.

"Yes, but that was a long time ago. Look how long it took me. I worked long and hard for ten years or more to get to the level that Anthony could get to in three years with the right connections. It's different now---different from when I was climbing the ladder. I just feel I know what's best for him. I'd like to talk to him when we have dinner tomorrow night."

"Be careful, John. Anthony is in love with Julie. I can tell. He doesn't want to disappoint you, but please don't make his life miserable at this point. Just let things progress. Chances are they'll end up going their separate ways. They're both so young and long-distance relationships rarely work out anyway. Julie will be here with all of those handsome senior boys and Anthony will be among hundreds of gorgeous girls at the university. Why don't you leave it alone?" she said almost pleading with him.

He thought about what she said and decided to wait to see how the conversation went when they saw Anthony. Then he thought about the letter again. He didn't open it, but felt it probably contained the usual 'love letter' messaging. He lifted the top off the red porcelain urn on his office shelf and placed it inside.

Chapter 7
Conversation with Anthony

Anthony's parents arranged to meet him at a nice, quiet restaurant. The food was great and there was plenty of laughter. At some point, his father brought up attending his company's fall stockholders' dinner which would take place sometime in October. Mr. Adkins really wanted Anthony to attend, because he wanted him to meet Marilyn Kennedy. He had arranged for Marilyn to attend with several other people who had large investments with his firm. *If I can just get Anthony to meet Marilyn, they might click. She is beautiful,* he thought.

"I'd like to attend if it works out with my schedule," Anthony responded thinking in the back of his mind that maybe he could see Julie while he was there. He didn't know that she was moving to Connecticut yet. The letter that was supposed to be hand-delivered by his friend Albert got waylaid and ended up in his father's red, porcelain urn in his office. "I'd like to take Julie to the dinner if you think that is appropriate," Anthony asked.

"Son, I don't think that is the best thing. You'll be meeting different people all night long---mainly men who are in the field you're going into, so she might find that a little boring. I'll be pulling you from person to person all evening," his dad explained. "And, what if you met a really wealthy young girl who could jumpstart your career? That couldn't be a bad thing."

I'm not interested, Anthony thought.

As the time got nearer, Anthony tried to contact Julie with no success. He finally decided to just surprise her when he arrived home. After all, if something came up and he couldn't make it, he wouldn't want to disappoint her. He didn't know that the Johnson's had already moved to Connecticut.

2

Anthony flew home to attend the dinner with his father. He barely arrived in time to catch a ride home from the airport and take a shower to get ready for the dinner. The dinner was on a Friday night, so he arranged to stay until Sunday afternoon to spend time with Julie. He would surprise Julie Saturday morning.

The dinner was everything his father said it would be. He mingled with his father's co-workers and met many influential people in the community. With less than a year left of school, he needed to make as many connections as he could. Then his father introduced him to Marilyn.

"Anthony, this is Marilyn Kennedy. She is here with her parents and some of our strongest investors. Why don't you spend a few minutes with them at this table, then I'll whisk you away to meet other people," his father said knowing he would leave Anthony there for as long as he felt he could.

Marilyn was, indeed, a beautiful young woman. She was a sophomore at Vanderbilt University and was as classy as she was smart. Her beautiful, almost black hair hung down to the middle of her back and her eyes were a deep, deep blue. She was very social and extremely extroverted---confident in all of her actions. She immediately felt attracted to Anthony---but then, what girl wouldn't be!

"Anthony, would you please take a picture with me? The photographer is coming to our table. I'm dying to be in a picture with such a handsome man," she asked as she cuddled his arm and pulled him up close to her.

Anthony didn't really feel like he had a say in the idea. He was whisked away for her beloved photo-op. *She's not Julie*, he thought while he smiled for the camera. His father looked on from across the room and smiled.

The photographs from the evening were being picked up by the local newspaper, so in a few days, Anthony's picture with Marilyn cuddled up to him and smiling brightly was on one of the inside social sections. He didn't even think about that at the time. He really didn't think of anything other than how glad he was going to be to see Julie the next day. Unfortunately, he was in for a big surprise!

Chapter 8
Julie Has Moved?

Anthony tried to call Julie, but the home phone was disconnected. *How can that be?* He thought. *It must be a problem with the line. I'll just drive over to her house. I hope she's there and not off on some track meet somewhere.*

When he got to her house, he saw a For Sale sign in the yard. *What? This makes no sense. If they were moving, I'm sure Julie would have written me and told me. Maybe they just moved into another house?*

He ran down to the post office to see if there was a forwarding address. There wasn't. At least there wasn't one yet---it hadn't been processed. Julie's parents were late in giving the forwarding address because of all of the confusion in the rush of moving.

Arriving back home, he felt really depressed. For the first time, he felt that maybe Julie didn't have the same feelings for him that he had for her. There would be no other way to explain it. *What am I going to do?*

He asked around to as many people as he could find to inquire about where the Johnson family had moved. He finally found one of Julie's track buddies downtown. "Do you know where Julie moved to? I saw the 'For Sale' sign on her house," he asked in almost a panic.

"Yeah, Julie and her parents moved to Connecticut. It was a really quick move. We didn't even know about it until it had happened. I don't have her phone number, but I know I have an address somewhere in my purse----here—here it is. Let me give this to you," she said trying to be helpful.

Anthony took the small piece of paper and guarded it like it was really valuable. It *was* really valuable to him. It was the only link he had to connect with Julie.

He went home, wrote a letter, and then left it on the kitchen counter, so his mother could mail it. He needed a stamp but then it could just go out to the mailbox and the mailman would pick it up. It read:

Dear Julie,

I just found out that your family has moved to Connecticut! I didn't know until I came in for a special dinner for my father's company and had trouble reaching you. The phone had been disconnected and now I understand why. I went to your old house and saw the 'For Sale' sign.

Julie, I still love you very, very much. I don't know if you decided to quit communicating because you want to move on with your life or what. Maybe you have found someone else? I never heard from you

*once I arrived at the university. So, I am going to
leave the ball in your court. If you want to continue
this crazy, long-distance relationship then let me
know one way or another. IF I don't hear, I will
know your answer.*

We will be together (I hope) someday-----I promise.

*Love,
Anthony*

Since Julie wasn't there, Anthony felt like he didn't
have anything else to do. He wasn't interested in
hanging out with anyone other than his parents, so
they had plenty of time to talk. He told them about
Julie moving. They had not heard that, but his
father actually liked it. He didn't show it around
Anthony, but he was still interested in Anthony
being with Marilyn and this would make his plan
soooo much easier.

Anthony was depressed and it was noticeable. He
just wasn't the happy, cheerful guy anymore.

His mother found a postage stamp, placed it on the
letter, and walked it out to the mailbox. She felt so
sorry for Anthony. She convinced him to go to the
store with her, mainly to give him a change of
scenery. Being at home gave him too much time to
think about Julie. She wanted to buy groceries and
prepare his favorite dinner in hopes of cheering him
up.

After they left for the grocery store, his father walked out to the mailbox, retrieved the letter, and added it to the red, porcelain urn in his office. He felt a little guilty but convinced himself that what he was doing was in the best interest of his son. He knew what was good for Anthony----he thought.

Anthony tried to act cheery at dinner especially since his mother tried so hard to give him everything he loved to eat that he couldn't get in his dormitory. He actually only barely remembered the meal. He was so concerned about Julie that his worry overcame everything. *Did I do something wrong? Did I take Julie for granted? Did I misread her interest in me? I know she was interested but with us being apart, maybe someone else walked into her life. I wouldn't doubt it.*

Chapter 9
Picture in the Newspaper

Meanwhile, Julie was thinking almost the exact same thing. She waited for him to respond to her letter. He never responded, because he never got the letter. She didn't know that, however. After all, she thought it had been hand-delivered. He would *have* to get it. She didn't respond to Anthony's letter, because she didn't get his letter, either.

Then something happened to cause Julie emotional pain. The community newspaper that her parents had before they moved was mailed to their new home. It always arrived about a week late because of the mail, but they always got it. Julie generally didn't pay too much attention to it, but on this particular day, Julie *did* glance at the newspaper. In the social events section was the picture of Anthony at his father's company dinner. He was smiling and Marilyn was snuggled up to him, holding his arm and leaning into him. The caption to the picture said, "Up and coming Anthony Adkins with his special date." The newspaper got that wrong. She wasn't his date. He didn't even think she was special!

Julie's mother saw her stare at the picture and couldn't stand the pain that her daughter was experiencing. She hugged her daughter but couldn't say a word. There was nothing to say.

The next week when the newspaper arrived, Julie's mother quickly thumbed through the little paper to the society section. Sure enough----another picture of Marilyn standing beside Anthony. If she had read the caption, she would have realized it was another picture from the same dinner as the week before, but she didn't. All she could think about was getting the paper out of the house. She did not want Julie seeing a picture of Anthony and Marilyn *again*. Gloria rolled the paper up, walked out to the garbage can, and threw it in. *Whew! Got rid of that!*

She never knew that Julie accidentally saw it when she went to the garbage can to throw out the trash from her bedroom. Glancing down, she noticed the newspaper and felt she had to retrieve it. She realized that her mother, more than likely, threw it away, so she wouldn't see it. That really piqued her curiosity. Sneaking the paper into her room, she opened it to the society section and there it was---- another picture of Anthony with Marilyn. She closed the paper without reading the caption. That's the day she tried to close the book on her relationship with Anthony. It was just too painful.

Chapter 10
Mr. Adkins's Strategic Planning

With the relationship between Julie and Anthony being strategically derailed, his father proceeded in pushing Anthony toward Marilyn Kennedy. He even went so far as to discuss the potential relationship between Anthony and Marilyn with Marilyn's father! They knew each other well, and both thought it would be a great partnership---marriage.

Mr. Adkins made sure Anthony had plenty of opportunities to see and be around Marilyn. And somewhere along the way, she decided that she was going after Anthony on her own. Prior to him, every other young man chased after Marilyn and tried to pressure her. Anthony was totally opposite. He basically showed her NO attention. He certainly didn't run after her. He hadn't gotten over Julie. He wasn't interested in Marilyn. That did it—she was going after him. Now it became a challenge. *I always get everything I want, and if I want Anthony then I'm going to have him. He may not know it yet, but he'll find out*, she thought to herself.

Anthony's father even went so far as to tell him some very disturbing news. "Anthony, someone came into the office who was one of Julie's friends at school. She said she heard Julie was getting married." There was no friend. There was no engagement. But with that news, Anthony tried to

get Julie out of his mind. It was just too sad. He
had to quit thinking about her.

2

Marilyn chased after Anthony and was unrelenting
in her pursuit. She always got everything she
wanted, and this wasn't going to be any different.
Finally, Anthony gave in. His father tried to
convince him that if he married Marilyn, everything
would be absolutely great. He wasn't convinced,
but if he couldn't be with Julie, then he really didn't
care one way or another. He really didn't.

The engagement came. Anthony never really
believed that Marilyn loved him. He even thought
that she all she really wanted was a really big social
event where she could be the center of everyone's
attention. He didn't care. *Just go with the flow,* he
thought.

Marilyn also decided that she was not going to take
Anthony's name. When he asked her why not, she
said, "I've always loved my name, Anthony. I like
names like Kennedy, Vanderbilt, Rockefeller,
Biltmore, Worthington, and Remington. They just
sound so sophisticated. You really don't mind, do
you?"

Well, yes, he did. Every woman he knew took her
husband's name. But, then again, did he *really* care?
He didn't care enough to have a discussion with

Marilyn. *I bet Julie would take my name and be very proud to do so*, he thought.

3

Anthony's father was right about one thing. After graduating and getting started in his profession, Anthony's business soared. Not only did he get huge investment money from Marilyn's parents, but almost every relative and family friend loaded him up. In no time at all, he had quite a reputation in the finance field.

It's not that Anthony needed to make millions of dollars. Marilyn was the recipient of a trust fund of over twenty-three million dollars, so money flowed freely. Marilyn's goal in life was to throw as many large parties as possible, wear as many expensive designer clothes as possible, carry designer handbags worth thousands of dollars, and drive the most expensive cars. She felt that life would be so boring if she didn't take several trips a year to England, Italy, and Spain. Shopping trips to New York were scheduled monthly.

Anthony was highly successful and his portfolio was massive. But it didn't make him happy.

With each and every year, Marilyn wanted more and more. Soon, they owned mansions across the world, a Lear Jet at their disposal, and a Rolls Royce. They never drove it because they both preferred other vehicles, but she wanted one, nonetheless. It was all about showing others what they had. Anthony just went along with it. It was easier than arguing.

The extravagance was bad enough. But what Marilyn insisted on was that Anthony escort her to at least three or four social events *every* week. Then there were the galas, the banquets, the operas, the fundraisers. He was living in his tuxedo.

Since Anthony had always wanted to have a family, he asked Marilyn when they should start planning for children. She looked at him like he was crazy. "When would we possibly have time to have children? We have so many important projects that we have to work on. I couldn't possibly ignore my fundraising commitment. I just can't see myself staying at home with screaming 'brats,' can you?"

That's not what Anthony wanted to hear, but thinking about it, he didn't think Marilyn would make a good mother, anyway. He knew she wouldn't give up anything that makes her happy. She would hire a nanny to do all the 'mother' things. Anthony didn't want that for any child.

Anthony managed to keep so busy with his work and their social events that 15 years went by without noticing. Then something really terrible happened---really terrible.

Chapter 11
The Accident

One night when Anthony was rushing to get to the biggest fundraiser of the year, a large transport truck ran through a red light and crashed into Anthony's car. It took more than an hour just to get Anthony out of the wreckage; his car was crushed. He was rushed to the hospital where his injuries were so critical, that he was not expected to survive.

"This is terrible," Officer Moran said shaking his head. He knew Anthony fairly well. Talking to another officer, he said, "Anthony Adkins is one of our most prominent citizens. He is highly successful, but what I know about him is that he is very generous. He has helped out the police department for many, many years. Anytime we needed anything, he was the first to help out. I sure hope he pulls out of this. I think he was on his way to the fundraiser at the Hilton. We better word get to his wife.

They immediately drove to the fundraiser to notify Marilyn of the accident. "Mrs. Kennedy, I'm Officer Moran. I'm sorry, but your husband has been in a very serious accident and he is in the hospital. You need to go immediately," the officer said. He knew it was more than a serious accident but didn't want to tell her that. He felt she would go to the hospital immediately anyway, so he decided to tell her as little as possible.

"Is it really important that I go right now? I'm being honored on stage in about 15 minutes, and I hate to miss out on that," she said without even asking the officer about the accident or how badly Anthony was injured.

"You need to go NOW," he replied not expecting her reactions.

"OK, officer. I'll go now. Thank you for telling me." She had no intention of missing out on being recognized on the stage with the possibility of a standing ovation. *I'm sure Anthony will be ok. He's strong. It's only 15 minutes. I'll go after the award.*

Marilyn didn't get to the hospital until after the fundraiser was finishing up.

2

Anthony was in a coma for seven days, and then his kidneys started shutting down. Because of his injuries, one kidney had to be removed. His doctors didn't know if the other kidney would survive, or if he would have to be on dialysis for the rest of his life. A successful kidney transplant would be a blessing, but kidneys were hard to come by.

The word got out that Anthony was in critical condition and desperately needed a donor kidney. Almost all of Anthony's relatives and many of his friends had blood and tissue tested for compatibility measures. There was also a national donor organization that had a data bank for transplants of all kinds.

Weeks went by. Anthony's health was failing. There was the fear that Anthony would not last long enough to receive a transplant. He was placed on dialysis. With dialysis, he was able to barely stay alive.

3

Anthony had plenty of time to think about his life. Here he was--one of the wealthiest men in the country--lying in a hospital bed, working to get his life back. All the money in the world couldn't really help him now. He continued his dialysis treatments, but his body didn't respond as well as the doctors had hoped. If they could just keep him going until a kidney came in! Unfortunately, they saw too many patients die waiting for a kidney. Even if one were donated to Anthony, there is no guarantee that it would take successfully, even if the match were perfect. There were so many variables to consider.

Anthony saw very little of Marilyn while he was in the hospital. She was just *so* busy with all of her social activities. She still felt the shopping trips to New York were necessary. She called him from New York when she was there and told him all about the things she had found, and what good deals they were. "Oh, Bachendorf's has the latest Chanel

bag! No one else has that one that I know of! I'm
so excited about it!" she exclaimed. She was
usually so excited that she'd forget to ask Anthony
has he was doing. He listened like any good
husband would do, but really, he couldn't care less.

Once, when she finally made it to the hospital, she
said, "Anthony, darling, I'm so sorry I haven't been
up here recently, but I knew you were getting the
best of care. There's nothing I can really do,
anyway. Right?   Are you feeling any better?"

Anthony could tell Marilyn was just there out of a
slight feeling of obligation, and she was chomping
at the bits to get out of there and on with her day.

"That's right. There's nothing you can do anyway.
I'll be fine," he said convincingly. *Life is too short.*
Mine may even be shorter than originally expected
now. I need to re-evaluate everything---my life
before the accident was not really a life at all.

4

Good news. The doctors came into Anthony's
room the very next morning and were excited to tell
him that a donor had been found.

"Your donor is a perfect match. We've gone
through the normal blood and tissue tests and
everything looks fine. This is a gift from heaven,
Anthony," Dr. Burton said with great excitement.
She saw it as Anthony's only hope for leading a

normal life again. If the donor kidney were accepted by Anthony's body, then he wouldn't have to remain on dialysis and he could lead a normal life. Even though he would have to remain on anti-rejection medication for the rest of his life, that was nothing compared to being tied to the dialysis machines all the time.

"Do you know who the donor is? Did someone die or did someone just donate a kidney? Don't most kidneys come from accident victims? Would I know if a living person donated the kidney?" Anthony asked one question after the other. His mind was whirling. "I was just wondering if any of my friends or relatives matched."

"We don't know. All we can tell you is there were no family members who matched, because those are checked first," the doctor answered.

Surgery was scheduled for April 13. *Lucky 13, I guess,* Anthony thought. Thirteen had always been a very lucky day for him. In fact, he was born on the thirteenth, his mother and father were born on the thirteenth, and his niece and brother-in-law were also born on the thirteenth. Two of his best friends also had birthdays on the thirteenth. His uniform number when he played basketball was thirteen. His office extension number was thirteen. He won a lottery on a chartered flight to Las Vegas and won thirteen $100 bills. Several of his rental properties had address numbers that added up to the number thirteen. The last four digits of his home phone number added up to the number thirteen. It was just uncanny how many times the number thirteen crept into his life. Now, he may actually get his life back on the thirteenth if the kidney transplant works!

One of his close friends, a friend who also went through the procedure to be a possible donor, had a birth certificate printed up with the date of the transplant---April 13---as Anthony's birthdate. In a way, it *was* his second birthdate. The birth certificate was framed and Anthony kept it in his office.

On the morning of his transplant, he had time to think through his life. He thought about the time he had with Julie. He thought about how their lives diverged to the point what where they were going on separate paths. He was sad. He thought about his life with Marilyn. He realized that he was never happy---not even at the beginning of his marriage to her. *Why did I let others guide me instead of doing what I really wanted to do? Maybe I felt that without Julie it really didn't matter anyway. I also think that I just wanted to make my father happy. If I survive this transplant, I'm going to change my life.*

The transplant was very successful. In a short period of time, Anthony was almost back to full health. However, he would need to remain on anti-rejection medication for the rest of his life. That was a small price to pay for getting his life back. He felt that he was getting a second chance at living

and he would be indebted to the donor for life.
How could he ever repay the donor or the donor's
family? He didn't even know who the donor was.

5

Anthony felt that he had changed considerably after
the transplant. Maybe it happened because he came
close to facing death? He knew that his life had to
change.

He realized he couldn't take it any longer. He
couldn't take all the nightly events and the tuxedos.
He couldn't take the banquet food and drinking. He
couldn't take the useless chit-chat of Marilyn's
friends. Besides, he didn't really believe that
Marilyn loved him. One day he asked her,
"Marilyn, do you love me?"

"Well, of course I love you----you're my husband,"
she answered acting somewhat annoyed.

"No, Marilyn. That's not what I'm asking. Do you
really love me?" he asked again very seriously.

Looking straight at him she answered, "Yes---yes---
oh,--- *whatever*." Then she turned and left the room.

That's all he needed. He knew if two people are in
love, really in love, no one needed to ask. It's
automatically felt. He didn't feel it and neither did
she. He moved out and they became officially
separated. Marilyn didn't seem to care. As long as

she had her designer clothes, her designer bags, her Mercedes, her Rolls Royce in the four-car garage, and the Lear jet for her trips around the world, she was fine.

Chapter 12
Letters in the Red Urn

After moving out of the 13,800 square foot mansion that Anthony and Marilyn bought together, he bought a very modest house and enjoyed it very much. It was a three-bedroom, two bath house that had a two-car garage. There was a cozy fireplace in the corner of the family room. The fireplace in the mansion was huge and no matter how large the fire was, there was no feeling of coziness. The room was just too large; the furniture was too far from the fireplace. It was so different in Anthony's little house. The room was cozy---the fireplace was warm and inviting---the flames danced and changed colors. Anthony loved every minute he spent in that room. *How can houses be so different? How can feelings be so different?* There were times when Anthony placed a quilt on the floor in front of the fireplace, lay down, and soaked up the warmth.

His kitchen was probably one-fifth the size of the kitchen in the mansion, but it had everything he needed---one double-sink instead of two double sinks on an island, one oven instead of two double ovens, one dishwasher instead of two, one microwave instead of two, one small pantry instead of a large walk in pantry with an appliance island. When Anthony cooked soup, or made a brisket, or cooked hamburgers, or even just made a sandwich, he had plenty of space. In fact, it was easier----fewer steps between the refrigerator, sink, oven, and stove. He had a two-car garage instead of a four-car garage. Anthony gave his Jaguar to Marilyn. He took their Toyota pickup. In the mansion, Marilyn had her Mercedes, he had the Jaguar, the Rolls Royce sat in the garage unless Marilyn wanted to really impress someone, and the pickup sat in the garage until he needed to deliver something for a charity event. Anthony actually preferred driving the pickup everywhere, but Marilyn wanted him to always be seen in the Jaguar. Appearance was everything to her. So now, he used his pickup all the time, and if he parked it in the garage, he still had plenty of room on the other side of the garage for storage. With every day that went by, he appreciated his little house more and more. It really became a 'home' to him. He was as happy as he could be leading a quiet life.

When his workday was over, he actually looked forward to being at home. He pulled his suit off when he got home and put on sweat pants and a sweat shirt. He thought back to what he used to do in his previous life-----come in from work, take off the suit, take a shower, put on the tux and walk out the door. In his new life, he treasured every minute that he had to walk out in the back yard, putter around the house, walk around the neighborhood, or just watch television. When the days were cold, he looked forward to sitting in front of the fireplace while reading a book. *Life is so nice---life is so nice----thank you donor for giving me another life.*

He spent more and more time with his parents. They were getting older and needed more assistance. Then his mother became very ill. Anthony was glad that he was able to help her as much as he did. There were days when all he did was talk to his mom. She seemed to need to talk. Maybe he did, too.

On one particular day, the conversation turned to Anthony's life with Marilyn. Mrs. Adkins said, "Son, your dad thought he was doing the best thing for you many years ago, when he pushed you toward a life with Marilyn. He didn't think your relationship with that high school girl would last anyway, so he seemed to be on a mission. I think over the years, he felt that maybe he did the wrong thing. He knew you wanted a family, and you were never given that opportunity. He knew you weren't one who wanted a high society life, but yet you were living that life, too. He looked at your life and always wondered about what he did. He always felt that he made the right decision concerning your business, and you were certainly more successful than he was at your age, but later in life he saw that money isn't the answer to everything. Parents make mistakes, Anthony. I've certainly made a lot of mistakes in my life, too. We can't change that now, but we can look forward. Anthony, decide how you want to live the last forty to fifty years of your life and do it."

After the death of his mother, his father's health failed steadily. Mr. Adkins left the hospital to spend his final days at home. Anthony set up a hospital bed in his father's bedroom and hospice workers helped out every day. Mr. Adkins hallucinated often because of the medication administered to eliminate his pain.

Some days, he thought gnats were swarming in his room. He swatted at them and sometimes tried to blow them away. When the doctor dropped by to check on him, Mr. Adkins said, "Don't you see them, doctor?" He acted puzzled that the doctor couldn't see the gnats swarming.

On another day, he thought he was flying in a plane. He looked out the window and acted like it was the window of an airplane. He talked about how smooth the flight was.

On the last day of his life, Anthony's father mumbled more than normal. "Dad, what are you saying? Dad, can you hear me?"

"I'm sorry-----sorry-----I was ---wrong---was wrong---I love you----forgive me son----son---- forgive me----red ---red urn---I'm sssorry," his father whispered. Anthony couldn't actually understand what his father meant. He heard the words, but his father was slurring so much. And he just didn't understand. *Why is dad apologizing to me? What is he talking about?*

Then his father closed his eyes and his heart stopped. Anthony lay his head on his father's chest and cried.

3

After the funeral, Anthony spent the next few weeks giving away the furniture in the house and all of the kitchen items. When he was cleaning out his father's office at home, he saw the red urn on the shelf and remembered his father mumbling the day of his death about the red urn. Anthony had forgotten about it!

He picked up the urn, set it on the desk and then lifted the lid. He reached inside and pulled out two faded envelopes. They were letters….unopened letters. The first letter was addressed to him with Julie's return address on the front. At the bottom she printed 'personal.' It was still sealed. The second envelope was addressed to Julie at her new home in Connecticut. Anthony recognized it was his handwriting. It was sealed also.

Anthony sat down at the desk and carefully opened Julie's letter.

Dear Anthony,

What a shock! My father was offered the promotion of a lifetime by the president of his company. My parents said that I could finish out my senior year by living with my Aunt Gena, but I just didn't want to spend the last year I may have with my parents away from them. My biggest concern is being farther away from you. When you return for Thanksgiving, I won't be there. I won't be there for Christmas, either. Would you consider visiting me and my family in Connecticut for Thanksgiving or Christmas or both? I love you and can't stand the thought of being away from you that long. There's also the possibility of spending next summer with Aunt Gena before we both go to the university. Your last year will be my first year.

However, I may be expecting too much. I don't want to take you for granted. If you think this long-distance relationship can work out, please get back to me. If you don't want this, I will understand.

I thank God every day that we got to be together last summer. I have never been happier in my life. But the decision needs to be yours. I'll wait to hear.

> *I Will Always Love You...I Promise*
> *Julie*

His heart ached. He couldn't believe what he was reading---or really he could. He knew that was exactly how they felt about each other in those days.

But he never got that letter. If he had just known!!
Then he opened the letter that he had written to her.
He read:

Dear Julie,

*I just found out that your family has moved to
Connecticut! I didn't know until I came in for a
special dinner for my father's company and had
trouble reaching you. The phone had been
disconnected and now I understand why. I went to
your old house and saw the 'For Sale' sign.*

*Julie, I still love you very, very much. I don't know
if you decided to quit communicating because you
want to move on with your life or what. Maybe you
have found someone else? I never heard from you
once I arrived at the university. So, I am going to
leave the ball in your court. If you want to continue
this crazy, long-distance relationship then let me
know one way or another. IF I don't hear, I will
know your answer.*

We will be together (I hope) again-----I promise.

> *Love,*
> *Anthony*

Anthony knew exactly what had happened. He
knew his father had kept the letters from them to
control their relationship. Thoughts swirled in his
head---confusing thoughts.

Anthony cried. Both he and Julie wanted to continue their relationship and it didn't happen. But what was *extremely* hurtful to Anthony was the fact that his *own father* kept the letters from reaching their destination. His life would have been different, if he had read that letter.

He had to find Julie. He had to see her...and he had to talk to her. He had to look into her eyes.

But what if Julie is in a happy relationship? If so, I won't tell her about the letters. I don't want to disrupt her life---I just have to find out for myself.

Just the thought of seeing Julie again made him so excited that he couldn't sleep at night. He was fully prepared if he found out that she was happily married with several kids. He understood that. But, he had to find out.

Chapter 13
Julie's Life

After Anthony did not respond to the letter she
wrote telling of her family's move to Connecticut,
and his attempt to contact her was also sabotaged,
and then the picture in the newspaper of Anthony
with Marilyn Kennedy, Julie resolved herself to the
fact that she would never be with him. She needed
to build a life of her own.

Her baby boy was born on April 23 weighing
exactly seven pounds. Julie named him Alek
Anthony Johnson. He was such a good baby, never
crying and always cooing. Julie was an extremely
proud parent and her parents couldn't be happier.
They knew it would be harder for Julie to attend
college classes, but they were there to help. It was
so nice having a little baby in their home, again.

Julie decided to postpone college until Alek reached
school age. Once he went to kindergarten, she
would be able to attend her classes while he was at
school, and she would be there to pick him up after
school every day. She treasured the time that she
got to spend with him. In some ways, she was both
mother and father to Alek. Of course, her parents
were always there, so there was an element of male
influence around him, also. Her parents adored him
and he knew it. He pretty much had them wrapped
around his little finger.

Julie thought back to her childhood. She remembered 'playing school.' She took advertisements that came in the mail and used them for her 'school papers.' The junk mail sometimes had application pages that her 'student' had to fill out because the pages were the 'tests.' Then Julie graded the 'tests' and actually recorded the 'grades' in her gradebook---a spiral notebook. In elementary school, Julie and her friends placed 'school' at recess. *Really? You're in school and then you play 'school?' Teachers are born, I guess.*

Wanting to be an elementary school teacher, Julie thought working with Alek would be the perfect practice for later when she would actually have a job. She read books to him so often that some of the pages were almost worn out. The first thing he wanted when he got a bottle was to have a book read to him while he sipped.

Julie had always heard that phonics was the best program to help children learn to read. So, when Alek was only eighteen months of age, she had him identifying all of the sounds of the alphabet. Along with, "What sound does a dog make?" and "What sound does a cow make?" she asked, "What sound does a 'T' make?" or "What sound does a 'B' make?" In no time at all, he was making all the sounds. He thought it was a game. All the adults laughed at the sound of this little eighteen-month old makes the sounds of the letters. And he milked it for all it was worth! He loved attention.

Since he knew all of the sounds of the letters, both vowels and consonants, Julie decided to teach him some words. She started with the word 'cat,' then added 'dog' and 'pig.' Alek could easily spell those words. Soon, he was begging his mother to spell more and more words. When Julie was in the kitchen preparing a meal, Alek would ask, "Mommy, how do you spell farmer? How do you spell tiger? How do you spell…….whatever word he could think of at the time. So, Julie's plan was to write the words on index cards so he could play with the words. In no time at all, there was a tall stack of cards with words on them. The next thing they did together was make sentences by laying the cards down in order on the floor or on the couch. Soon, Alek was making really long sentences with his stack of cards. He loved playing this game. He was just two weeks shy of his third birthday! Julie made a note that when children know the sounds of the letters, words come quickly, then sentences follow.

These games led to Alek reading books on his own. Julie couldn't buy enough books for him. Then one day when he was four years old, Julie's cousin came to visit. Julie had told her about Alek's reading ability but she probably didn't believe it. She was an elementary school teacher and had been one for over fifteen years. She asked Julie if she could take Alek into the other room to let him read to her.

When they returned, Julie's cousin was shaking her head.

"Well, I can tell you that Alek reads better than any of my fifth graders!" she said smiling widely. "He never missed a word and read very fluently. I'm amazed."

Then the challenge came. "Alek," Julie said. "If you can spell the word 'pregnancy' I'll buy you a new t-shirt. Alek spelled the word without even thinking about it. "Ok, how about 'memorandum?' Julie knew he wouldn't get that one. But he did. "How about 'tongue?' He got it also. *How in the world did he get 'tongue?' That can't be sounded out phonetically!* She didn't remember how many words he ended up spelling correctly, but she knew she lost the bet----many times over.

3

To help Alek go to sleep at night---his bed was still in her bedroom---she'd make up stories to tell him. Every night he wanted her to tell him stories until he fell asleep. She became really weary of making up stories about dogs and cats and witches and ghosts. She decided to tell him stories about educational topics, like photosynthesis! *Doesn't that sound interesting?*

OK, Alek. I'm gonna to tell you a story about photosynthesis. When a green plant is growing, it needs food and water just like we do. It gets the water from the ground through its roots. Do you remember seeing the roots of the weeds when we pulled them up that day? Well, the water goes up the roots to the stem and it goes to all of the parts of the plant. When the sun shines, the sun hits the leaves and there is green stuff (she couldn't think of a better word to use) called chlorophyll. Chlorophyll combines with the water to form the food for the plant. When the plant has enough food, it can grow, just like you do. Oh---the plant also has to breathe. It doesn't breathe oxygen like you and I breathe but it breathes in carbon dioxide. When it breathes OUT, it breathes out oxygen! What's interesting is that WE breathe in oxygen and we breathe OUT carbon dioxide. See, it's perfect. We breathe in what they breathe out and they breathe in what we breathe out. So, wouldn't it be good to have plants in our house? Everyone would be happy!

On another day, Julie taught Alek about the natural food chain. He was really excited to hear that the story wasn't about a chain but was about animals eating smaller animals or sharks eating smaller fish. "Ok, Alek, plants and grass grow in the dirt. Little bugs eat the plants and grass. Then a bird comes along and eats the bug that at the plant. A bigger bird comes along or maybe a bobcat comes along and eats the bird that ate the bug that ate the plant. Are you following me?" she noticed he was so interested in the food chain story. "OK, the bobcat is then eaten by a larger animal like a lion."

"Who eats the lion?" Alek asked patiently.

"Good question! I don't know. I think that is the end of the chain. We need to research that." Julie answered. She always said they needed to research the topic when she didn't have the answer. And she often didn't have the answer.

Dinosaurs were also an interesting topic for his bedtime stories. Julie had to read up on some of the information just so she would get it right! He never tired of her educational stories. He was like a sponge, absorbing all the bits of knowledge and loving it. That could be why, when he was tested as a very young child, that he scored in the beyond the very superior range. One question he got right that Julie had no way of knowing where he picked it up was this: How many minutes are in three-fourths of an hour? He answered it correctly.

When he went to a private kindergarten class, he told the teacher that he knew Spanish. Then he proceeded to count in Spanish and say several Spanish words. Julie knew that she hadn't taught him that. *Where did he pick that up?* When she asked him, he responded that he learned it on the television. He watched one of those children's shows every afternoon.

4

Alek was finally old enough to go to first grade, so Julie decided to start attending classes at the local community college. It was both convenient and inexpensive. In no time at all, she had her degree in elementary education and applied to local school districts for a job. She had always thought that a teaching job would be perfect for her, especially since she wanted to be available to take care of Alek during the various school breaks and in the summer. The summer was "their" time to be together the most.

At the beginning of Alek's first grade year, his teacher caught on quickly that he was very advanced. He could read fluently, of course, but when in the reading circle with the other children, he deliberately slowed down and read like they did, pausing more in between the words. He didn't want to be different. The teacher didn't want him to digress so she started sending him to the library. When she picked up that his math skills were also very advanced, she petitioned the school board to allow Alek to advance to the second grade. The district had a regulation in place that prohibited students from skipping grades. They believed students could be given enough individualized instruction to enrich their experiences at every grade. The teacher had Alek tested, so she would have information to provide to the school board. The reading teacher tested Alek and determined that his reading level for reading comprehension was eighth grade (that was the highest level this particular test evaluated) and his word reading level went beyond that level. The school board approved his moving to second grade when he was one of the youngest kids in first grade. Alek did fine in second grade which meant he would graduate from high school at the age of sixteen.

5

Alek started playing little league baseball when he got old enough. Then the entire family followed him around to his various games. No one cheered more loudly than Julie and her parents.

Elementary school led to middle school which then led to high school. No one could believe how quickly Alek was growing up. Everyone could see the resemblance he had to his father but really no one mentioned it. It was still painful for Julie even after all of those years.

When Alek started high school, everything started getting more difficult for him. He was very smart--- he had an IQ of 123, but he still struggled with many of his classes. He was such a good kid, and he wanted to do so well, but it was a struggle. Julie decided to hire a tutor to help him and to see if that would turn his grades around. After a few sessions, the tutor, Ms. Pickrel, had a discussion with Julie.

"Julie, when I work with Alek, I can see that he is suffering. He is trying his hardest to stay focused, but he keeps losing his attention. I've seen this time and time again. I really think he would benefit from ADHD medication. It would be a trial run at least, but maybe it will do the trick," the tutor explained.

"Oh," Julie said hesitantly, "I just really want to stay away from medication if at all possible. I think he needs to learn more self-discipline and self-control."

"Well, why don't you read through some of my books on attention deficit hyperactivity disorder? I think they might help explain what is going on," Ms Pickrel offered.

Julie took the books and read through them. Then she designed a program that Alek could follow at home and hopefully it would do the trick. She wanted him to study in his room for two hours every night even if he had nothing to turn in the following day. Just studying, in her mind, would be beneficial. If he did that, then he could do the other activities that he enjoyed doing.

When that didn't work as Julie had planned, she resorted to grounding him from his beloved truck. When Alek came home one day and said he was going to quit school as soon as it was allowed, she became really worried. Julie called Ms Pickrel and asked her what to do. She was ready to try anything. Ms Pickrel referred her to a medical doctor known for his expertise in ADHD.

After approximately one month of being on medication, Alek started making excellent grades and was, once again, happy with school. He started helping other students do well in their classes. He made good grades on all of his tests. One day, Alek showed Ms Pickrel an assignment that he had done that week in school. "Look, I did this assignment in only one class period!" He showed her a full page essay on one side and a very detailed drawing on the other side. He said, "I could have never done this before."

Before another tutoring session, Alek told Ms Pickrel that he made a 94 on his chemistry test and it was the highest test score out of all of the teacher's chemistry classes. "Now you'll have to become a doctor," Ms Pickrel said knowing Alek always wanted to become a doctor. "You can't make a 94 on your chemistry test and not become a doctor!

Alek became a different student while on medication. Ms Pickrel could see it clearly when she tutored him in geometry. Before, she saw that he struggled to stay tuned in. Before, he watched the clock, waiting for the session to end. He as getting his homework done, but it was no fun. On this particular evening, Alek was totally focused on learning his assignment. He was so focused that Ms Pickrel didn't tell him when the session had ended. She wanted to see just how long it would take him to figure out the hour was up. She wanted to see how long he could stay focused. It was not until fifteen minutes had gone by that he glanced at the clock. "Oh! I'm sorry! Our hour is over. I can't believe it went by so fast!" Alek said apologetically.

"Alek, I knew exactly what time it was, but because I don't have a student following you, I wanted to just see how focused you could be. This is great, Alek. You could have never done this before!" she replied enthusiastically.

"You know, if I had taken this medication my freshman year, I'm sure I would've done well instead of failing so many things," Alek mentioned.

"I'm sure you would have, but the most important thing now is that you are going to be fine. You'll be able to go to college, do very well, and go on to medical school like you have always wanted to do," Ms Pickrel said with a smile of her face.

6

When Alek was a junior in high school, he inquired about his father. When he saw how distraught it made his mother, and when he saw her eyes tearing up, he decided to never bring up the subject again. After all, he loved his family, and he didn't want to cause any heartache. All he knew was that his mother and father were never married, but that his mother loved his father deeply. He decided he would ask at a much later date, or maybe not at all.

Once when he was with his grandmother, he mentioned the topic. "Grammy, what do you know about my father?" Alek ventured out to ask one day when they were alone together.

"Alek, he was a wonderful man who loved your mother more than anything else in the world. Your mother made the decision a long time ago, before you were born, to raise you herself. I know it is very painful for her. Maybe someday she will tell you more. All I can tell you is that your father never knew you were born.

7

Alek grew up to be a fine young man. He attended a local university and majored in marketing. He met his future wife at the same university and they were actually married right before their senior year. Julie couldn't have been happier. Shortly after graduation, they settled into a small home and their first child, Andrew, was born. He looked so much like Alek's baby picture that it was uncanny. Just one year later, a baby girl came into the picture. They named her Cassie. Julie's family grew by three extra members quickly. Even though Julie's parents were getting older, they continued to help whenever they could.

Julie started painting after her son and his beloved married. Although she was still teaching, she had the summers free and extended time at Thanksgiving, Christmas, and Spring Break. She took art classes at the local hobby shop and managed to paint several things that she felt good about. Sometimes she painted animals, sometimes she painted landscape, but she really liked painting portraits the most. *Why do I pick the most difficult thing to paint?* She often wondered. Then she learned that using chalk, or pastel chalks, made drawing portraits much easier than oil paints. It was easier to blend the colors. Her teacher, Calonnie, taught her everything she needed to know.

Then Julie remembered that she has *always* drawn pictures. She didn't have to sit and read in the reading circle in first and second grade because the teacher had her in the back of the room drawing and coloring pictures. Everything she did in those days was Crayola drawings. In fact, Julie still has several pictures that she did while in first grade. She drew and colored historical figures when doing a project in eighth grade, but she never got serious about portraits until she bought a book about drawing portraits from photographs. That book gave her the knowledge and the talent to draw portraits that were pretty much on target. Then after retiring, she took lessons from Calonnie.

8

There was one time when a nice gentleman, Joseph, wanted to take Julie out for dinner. At first, she thought, *Why Not? My life has simplified since Alek married, and I actually have more time to do what I want.*

Julie and Joseph met when the school she worked at had an open house for parents. Although Joseph was not the parent of any of Julie's students, he noticed her on his way to his grandchild's classroom. He was actually there with his own daughter who quickly pointed out that Julie was a single teacher. Julie had many friends who were always working on getting her a boyfriend. Most of the time they were unsuccessful, but they wanted to try anyway. Julie was just too beautiful and too intelligent for her to remain single----or so they thought.

At the end of the open house, Joseph was introduced to Julie who looked radiant even after a long day of teaching. Joseph was immediately impressed. It took him no time at all to call her and ask if she'd go to dinner with him.

Joseph picked her up around 6:30 pm Friday evening and they drove to one of the finest restaurants in the city. He was the perfect gentleman. Although Julie was impressed with Joseph, she kept comparing him to Anthony without really meaning to do so.

The conversation was nice and quite interesting, but it wasn't like the conversation Julie had with Anthony when she first met him. As Joseph was talking, Julie found herself thinking of how funny Anthony was and how much they laughed together. She thought back to the dinner when she placed the penny on the tablecloth. When Anthony asked what that was, she explained that if the coin is heads up, it means: *I am thinking about you.*

"Did you always know you wanted to be a teacher?" Joseph asked sincerely. It was just regular conversation but at least she had a reply.

"Oh yes, I guess I knew I wanted to be a teacher from before I started elementary school," she answered, having her thoughts about pennies interrupted by his question.

"Were either of your parents school teachers?" Joseph asked as a follow-up to his earlier question.

Julie answered very politely and even tried to make her answer interesting. She, in turn, asked him typical 'get to know you' questions.

Even trying to keep the conversation going, Julie found herself thinking back to her time with Anthony. She remembered asking him if he ever murdered anyone or if he ever robbed a bank. The thought actually made her smile. Joseph thought she was smiling at him. She wasn't. The evening seemed to be rather long for Julie. She admitted that the food was excellent, that Joseph treated her like a queen, and that he was a true gentleman. He just wasn't Anthony.

Julie even gave the friendship another chance. The second date was going to be a double date with another friend of Julie's so she thought it would be fun. The two couples decided to go quite a bit more casual and have hamburgers and chocolate shakes at the local hamburger joint. Just having a female friend present enabled Julie to be more relaxed and less focused on memories from long ago. The evening went very well, and both couples seemed to be having a great time.

After the second dinner, Joseph made it clear that he wanted the friendship to develop into a more serious relationship. The conversation was interesting, but when she thought about it, she decided to discourage another date. She just couldn't think about being with any other man in a serious relationship-----ever. She dismissed any thought of being with a man, unless she could be with Anthony.

"Joseph, you are one of the nicest people I know. You are a total gentleman, and I admire everything that you have done in your life. You deserve a person who will devote her life to making you happy. I'm so sorry, but I'm not that person. It is not you. It is me. It wouldn't be truthful for me to go along with this relationship, if I know I can never fully commit to any man. Please believe that it is not you. You deserve so much more. I just don't want to waste your time---that wonderful woman is out there and you can find her." Julie did her very best to convince Joseph that it was her problem and not his.

Any other single woman would love to have Joseph asking her out and wanting a serious relationship. He is handsome, kind, honorable, and is a complete gentleman. In addition, like frosting on the cake,

Joseph owns his own company and is highly successful not only in his field but in the community as well.

After Julie had her conversation with Joseph, he took the 'mild' rejection very well. "Julie, I understand. I think you are a fantastic woman and you know exactly what is going to work for you. I respect that very much. Thanks for being honest with me. Just because we aren't going to go forward with a relationship, that doesn't mean we can't be friends. I'm here for you, if you ever need anything. Just call." Joseph meant every word that he said. Besides, he thought if she ever changed her mind, maybe it *would* work out.

That evening when Julie climbed into her bed to read a book, her favorite activity in the evening, she had a feeling of relief. She was relieved that she had handled the situation with Joseph in a way that left the door open to their friendship. She admired him but realized it was unfair to lead him on when she knew nothing could ever come from it. She made a note----*don't even go on a first date. It makes it more difficult in the long run.*

Chapter 14
Tragedy Strikes

Everyone seemed so happy. Life was good. Julie was pleased with her teaching position. She loved her students and felt that she was a good teacher for her students. Her son, Alek, was a dedicated husband and wonderful father to a little boy and a little girl. Julie was so proud. Then something terrible happened that turned Julie's whole world upside down.

Alek and his wife, Cathy, were visiting friends in another state when a terrible fire broke out in the middle of the night. Alek managed to get his children out safely even though he wasn't that familiar with the house. He thought Cathy was behind him, but then he didn't see her. He looked around frantically, but she wasn't anywhere in the yard. He had to go back in. When he went back in the house to get Cathy, part of the roof fell in on them. He and his wife were killed.

A police officer knocked on Julie's door early the following morning. She knew something was horribly wrong by the way the officer looked at her when she first opened the door. His face foreshadowed the pain he knew she would feel once he told her of her son's and daughter-in-law's deaths.

"I'm so very sorry, Ms Johnson…," and then he went on to tell her about the fire. Julie fell to her knees. *I always lose everything that means more than life itself to me. I can't bear this---not this time. God, help me!*

"What about the children? They have a one-year old girl and a two-year old boy. Are they OK? Please, God. Tell me they are OK," she cried uncontrollably.

"Yes, mam. They are both fine. Your son got them out of the house. He is a hero. They're being transported back here today. We'll bring them here as soon as they get back," the officer said sympathetically.

Julie was in a state of shock. Of course, she would take the children and raise them as her own. *But how do you take care of children when you don't see how you can function yourself?* The emotional pain she would face each and every day would be debilitating.

Although Julie didn't know how she was going to manage to put one foot in front of the other with the amount of sadness she was going through, she had no choice. Little Andrew and Cassie needed her. She would be there for them.

In reality, having the children helped her move on. She didn't have time to think----she didn't have time to worry----she didn't have time to cry. She had to become their mother *and* father. Her parents could help quite a bit, but they were getting older.

110

Julie decided to resign from her teaching position to stay at home with the children just like she stayed at home when Alek was young. It was going to be possible because of an insurance policy Alek had in place for his children. The way she figured, it would take care of them for five years. *Thank you, God.*

There were many nights when they all slept in Julie's bed. She needed to be close to them and they needed to be close to her. She wanted to give them all the closeness they needed. There were days they stayed in bed late and watched cartoons----laughing and laughing. Julie needed that, too.

Chapter 15
An Unexpected Visitor

Anthony was very happy in his single life, separated from his wife for over four years. He enjoyed living modestly and out of the "limelight." He never missed the banquets, the dinners, the fundraisers, and the travel. His favorite activity was having a greasy hamburger at the local hamburger joint and then going for a walk around the lake. *Life is good*, he often thought. *Life is not perfect, but it is good.*

He never quit thinking about Julie. He decided he was going to track her down. Even if she were happily married with several children, he just wanted to know if she were ok after all of these years.

Anthony asked several people until he was able to get Julie's parents' address. He didn't think Julie would be living there, but they would know how to find her for sure. Then it was up to him. He took the address provided and wrote her a letter addressed to her parents' home.

Dear Julie,

I know this letter is going to come as a surprise after all of these years. I just wanted to see if you and your husband would agree to have coffee with me, or lunch or dinner so that we could catch up on the past 20+ years. The last I heard was that you were getting married and had a child. I will be in your city in two weeks and I would love to see you. I will call you when I first get there to see if you are able to work some time into your schedule to meet. I hope this letter finds your parents well.

> *Sincerely,*
> *Anthony Adkins*
> *215-746-5503*

He read through the letter several times and then wadded it up and threw it into the trash. *This letter is dumb. I'm not going to send her this. I'm just going to show up and see if I can see her. I'll take my chances.*

2

Anthony walked up the sidewalk to the front door of the house that he hoped Julie's parents still lived in. He knocked on the door. The door slowly opened to reveal an older man, but it was clearly Julie's father.

"Mr. Johnson? I'm Anthony Adkins. I met you over twenty years ago when I dated Julie. I'm hoping you can tell me how I can find her? I'm here in town for about two weeks and I would love to meet her and her family," he said somewhat shyly. He really didn't know how Julie's father would take the idea of his wanting to find her.

"Anthony? Oh, sure! I remember you. Lots of years have gone by, huh?" he said jokingly. But in reality, Mr. Johnson was thrilled that Anthony was standing at his front door asking to locate his daughter. She had gone through so much emotional pain that any little ray of sunshine would be greatly appreciated. "I'll tell right where she is. Just go about three blocks down this street and then turn right at the corner where the park is. Her house is the third one on the left. Dang it, I don't know the number of the house, but you'll find it. It's the house with the red front door. It's the only house with a red front door, so you can't miss it. Hey--- glad to see you."

With that, Anthony turned and actually ran down the sidewalk to his car. He didn't want to waste one minute of time. *Three blocks, turn right by the park. Third house on Left. Red door. There it is!*

He parked at the curb and then walked up to the door. He knocked softly. Within seconds, the front door opened. At first, Julie just stared at him. He thought maybe she didn't recognized him. Actually, she did recognize him but didn't believe her eyes.

"Julie, I am going to be in town for a few days and I wanted to see you. You look absolutely gorgeous--- just like always," he said hoping to not scare her away.

"Well, I never remembered you being such a liar. As I recall, you were quite a respectable person,"

114

she said jokingly but with reservation. "Why don't you come in? I can offer you something to drink--- well, lemonade I mean."

"I'd love to," he said without hesitation. He walked into the living room and sat in one of the chairs near the sofa. Julie sat across from him in the other chair. *Am I really sitting here with Anthony?* She asked herself. *Am I dreaming?*

Both of them seemed a little nervous. Anthony thought Julie was married and Julie thought Anthony was married.

"How have you been, Julie?" he asked sincerely.

"Oh, I'm fine now. I lost my only son, Alek, and his wife, Cathy, about a year ago. There was a terrible fire and they were trapped inside. Alek managed to get his children out, but he and his wife died when the roof collapsed. How are your parents, Anthony?" she said wanting to change the subject from the fire.

"Oh Julie, I didn't know. I'm so sorry," he looked so sorrowful. His heart ached for her pain. "My parents have passed away. First, Mom passed and then less than a year later, my father passed away. At least, I was able to be with them for a few years before they died. I wouldn't trade that time with them for anything."

"I remember your parents well. They were good people," she said sincerely.

"Years ago, I had a terrible accident and had to have a kidney removed. The other one was also damaged and failed, so I almost died. I was on dialysis for several weeks and was going downhill when a donor kidney came in. My relatives and friends were tested for compatibility, but none were. I don't know who donated the kidney----don't really know if it were because of a death or what. I just know that my life was saved because of that. I have a lot to be thankful for. I think that scare made me reevaluate my life.

"Julie, are you still married to Alek's father?" he had to ask thinking it would open up the conversation and he'd find out more information.

"No, no. I'm not married to him," she answered truthfully. But she offered no more information.

"And are you still in love with him?" Anthony ventured to ask.

"Yes, Anthony. I am still very much in love with Alek's father----I always will be." Then in her mind she added, *I promise.*

Anthony's heart dropped. That wasn't what he wanted to hear, but he knew meeting with her might produce that kind of answer. He just had to find out one way or another and then get on with his life.

116

"I don't know why you are not married any longer, but I *do* understand about loving someone no matter what the circumstances," he replied sadly. He assumed she was married because that is what he had heard all those years ago. He just figured they divorced and she was still in love with her ex-husband.

Julie heard from time to time about Anthony and his wife, Marilyn. Their picture was always in the newspaper society section. She assumed they were still married. "Your wife is very lovely. I used to see pictures of the two of you from time to time."

Anthony seized the opportunity to tell her, "Julie, my wife and I have been separated for over four years. I moved back to our home town, so I could take care of my parents."

Julie was visibly shocked. All kinds of thoughts were going through her head. *Somehow, I have to tell him.* Then she said, "Anthony, would you please walk with me for a few minutes? I want to show you something."

"Sure, anything you want," he said as he helped her up from her chair and out the front door. They walked a few blocks down the street to the cemetery. Julie led him though the beautiful, scrolled-iron gate. In one of the most beautifully kept sections, Julie directed Anthony to Alek's gravesite.

Looking down at the headstone, thoughts flooded Anthony's mind. It read:

Alek Anthony Johnson
April 23, 1950   January 13, 1974

The first thing that attracted his attention was Alek's middle name. *Anthony* Anthony started thinking about the first date engraved on the headstone. *Julie and I were together intimately one time in July of that summer when we fell in love. She was never with any other person that I know of---I monopolized her time. Alek's middle name is Anthony? His last name is Johnson? She married someone with the last name of Johnson?*

"Julie, was there ever anyone else in your life after we met that summer? He had to ask.

"No. After we met there was *never* anyone in my life. I fell in love with you and there was never any other person," she answered truthfully.

"You said you love Alek's father?" he questioned.

"Yes, I do," she answered. She could tell he was really confused. "Anthony, *you* are Alek's father. I never married. If I couldn't have you, then I didn't want anyone."

All kinds of emotions flooded his mind. *My son. This is my son, but I never knew. How can I ever repay Julie for all of the pain I have caused her?*

"Julie, I am so sorry. I had no idea. I could have helped you. I could have ….." he said starting to cry.

"I know, Anthony. Maybe I did the wrong thing by keeping it a secret, but I thought it was the best thing for you. I couldn't bear the thought of your dropping out of school or being forced to shoulder the responsibility of a family while trying to finish school. I didn't want you to make your decision based on my needs. I'm sorry, too. Maybe I did the wrong thing."

Anthony put his arms around her, held her tightly, and they cried together. The sun was just starting to settle in the western horizon producing a hazy orange glow. "Let's walk back before it gets any later." They walked back holding each other as they walked.

Then Anthony told her about his father's plea on his deathbed. "My father asked me to please forgive him, telling me as best he could that he was wrong and he was sorry. He asked me to forgive him several times. He mentioned something about a red urn. At the time, I didn't understand why he was apologizing, so I credited it to hallucination. A few weeks later, when closing out the house, I remembered about the red urn. I found these letters inside."

Anthony pulled out the two, old, faded letters that he had found in his father's red porcelain urn. One was addressed to him; one was address to her. Reading the letters out loud, each of them realized how the letters had derailed the life that could have been. If it hadn't been for the undelivered letters and the deliberate miscommunication about each of their lives, they would have been together. From Anthony's father telling him Julie was married and expecting a child to the picture of Marilyn and Anthony in the paper at the social function saying she was his date. The history was all coming together---piece by piece.

"Julie, I believe we were meant to be together from the very first time we met. It was magical. But circumstances kept us apart. Please let me be a part of your life now," he pleaded.

"Oh Anthony, I love you as much today as I loved you almost twenty-five years ago. I never stopped loving you. I want us to be together, but I have my two young grandchildren now—Andrew is 3 and Cassie is 2. I'm all they have. I don't know how you feel about having little ones around at this time in your life," she said giving him an out if he needed it.

He looked straight into her eyes, "Julie, what you don't know is that I have wanted children, forever. I asked my wife about having children, but she was too busy for that. I didn't think I would ever experience being a father. If you will let me help you, I will be the happiest man alive. It would be the greatest gift anyone could ever give me."

"When do you want to start?" she asked laughing.

"Can I move in next week? All I need to do is pack up some things and I can be here---on full daddy duty," he said with a sparkle in his eye.

Am I dreaming? Julie asked herself. *I can't believe this. It feels like we are eighteen and twenty all over again. I don't feel a bit differently.*

3

They heard a knock on the door. It was Julie's parents bringing the children home from spending the day with them. They entered the house and started screaming as then ran up to Julie almost knocking her down. They wrapped their arms around her legs---one child on each leg.

"See what I mean?" Julie said to Anthony as her parents looked on laughing. "Are you strong enough to take this on?" Her parents were hoping they weren't reading too much into the interaction.

"Mom, Dad," she decided to explain. "I think you remember Anthony. Believe it or not, we are going to be together, finally. If you are shocked, I understand. I felt the same way only a couple of hours ago!"

"Mr. and Mrs. Johnson, Julie and I have pieced together our history over the past twenty years. We realized that unusual circumstances kept us apart. Julie can tell you all about it. But what's important now is that we have found each other again. It is a time in our life when we can finally be together. I have always wanted children and Julie needs help. She can't be both mom and dad. So here I am! With your permission, I will be moving here very soon."

Julie's parents were completely thrilled. They remembered Anthony very well. They knew Julie was totally in love with him but also thought that their lives had diverged naturally because of their youth. They didn't know that the relationship was derailed by outside forces. They would learn all about it, however.

4

Anthony was going to stay in town for a few more days, but with their new plans, he wanted to get back home to pack. He couldn't wait to start his new life with Julie. He also wanted to start divorce proceedings. Marilyn and Anthony had been separated for over four years mainly because she didn't want to have the title of divorcee. It was fine that their relationship was over with both of them, but they just didn't take the next step of actually divorcing. Now Anthony had the perfect reason for finalizing the paperwork. He wanted to start his new life with Julie.

Before Anthony left the next day for the airport, he found several Lincoln head pennies strategically planted by Julie. When he found one, he always said to himself, *I am thinking about you.*

Before he left, he held Julie in his arms. Julie told him, "I will always love you….I promise."

In return, he told her, "We will be together….I promise."

Chapter 16
Anthony's and Julie's Life Together

Things could not have been better for Julie and Anthony. It was like not *one day* had gone by since they met at the Dairy Queen more than twenty-five years ago. They joked and kidded just like before.

The children, Andrew and Cassie, seemed to make the adjustment of a new person in their lives very well. Being only two and three years old, they knew their mother and father were not with them, but they had always spent a lot of time with grandmother Julie so that was one element of their lives that was the same. They were not in their home they knew any longer, but Julie moved their furniture as well as all of their toys into her home to help with the transition. At first, they asked for their mommy and daddy which immediately brought tears to Julie's eyes, but she was learning how to deal with it. Every time she told them that their mommy and daddy were in heaven and that they would someday get to be with them again, it seemed to pacify them for a while. Over time, they asked less and less. Soon, instead of calling Julie "Mimi" like they had always done, they called her "Mommy." They also started calling Anthony "Daddy." He couldn't be happier.

Julie explained to Anthony that she was taking an extended leave from her teaching job so that she could take care of the children like she had done with their father. He agreed that was the perfect thing to do.

"I can financially handle being off work for a while because Alek had an insurance policy that will cover my house payments and our living expenses," she explained. She had always taken care of herself and she didn't even think about the fact that now there was someone else to help her with finances!

"Julie, I want you to take the money from the insurance policy and put it into a savings account for the children. You won't need any of it. What you don't know is that we will be fine financially. I won't be working, either, but we will have enough money. Don't worry," he said casually.

"But, I know you will be going through a divorce and some men really get beaten up during that process. Maybe you'll have other expenses or obligations. I just want you to know we won't be a burden to you," she said sincerely.

I guess Julie really doesn't know that Marilyn already had over twenty million dollars when we married and that my business made me equally as wealthy. Even though I gave Marilyn most of the mansions we had accumulated, and the Rolls Royce and the Lear jet, we are going to be great. Those things meant nothing to me----they were objects to give Marilyn self-worth and importance.

"Julie, is this house going to be big enough for our crew?" he asked her shortly after moving in. "I love your little house, but as the kids grow, they probably won't want to share a bedroom and knowing how girls can monopolize a bathroom, they probably need separate bathrooms," he mentioned over dinner with a laugh.

"I think you're right, Anthony, but for now I just love the coziness. We are all so close. I think the kids really like sharing twin beds in their bedroom. I hear them laughing a lot as they are going to sleep. They have lost so much in their young lives that I want to give them that closeness."

Every morning, the family shared breakfast together and then planned an activity. Some days when it was cold and dreary, they chose to stay inside, close to the fireplace. They cuddled up together under soft blankets to watch movies. Other days, when warm and sunny, they all went to the park to swing or play on the teeter-totters. The slides were a favorite of the children. Anthony even found out that he could go down the slide, also. He should have never done it the first time because then the children wanted him to slide with them every time. He was a little embarrassed when other parents came along with their children. They *did* look at him kind of strangely.

126

Julie had to work to keep Anthony from spoiling the children too much. He wanted to buy them everything! He wanted to give them everything! "Let's go get a banana split!" he'd said at the drop of a hat. Of course, the kids cheered, "Yes! Yes! Daddy, get 'nana spit.'"

Being financially secure, Julie and Anthony were able to spend all of their time with Andrew and Cassie. They wanted to spend as much time with them as possible knowing that when they had to attend school someday, things would change.

"Anthony," Julie said with a sense of seriousness. "I know you missed out on Alek's life. You would have made the greatest father to him. Because of my decision, you never knew him and he never knew you. I realize that was terribly wrong. But, I did what I thought was right at the time. Now, you are father to two babies---Andrew and Cassie. When I watch Andrew, I see Alek. He has the same mannerisms; he has the same personality. You are seeing Alek every day. He even looks at me the same way that Alek used to. He has Alek's blood, and he has your blood, and he has my blood. Someone in heaven was looking out for us when this reunion happened. I really believe that. I'm thankful for everything I have been given. I think of Alek every minute of every day, but I see him every minute of every day when I see Andrew."

Chapter 17
The Family Proposal

With Anthony's divorce finalized, he started making plans to marry Julie. Once he knew he and Julie would be together for the rest of their lives, he bought a very nice diamond ring. He didn't need her to see it or pick it out because he knew she would absolutely love it. He knew her so well.

At the jewelry store, he asked the salesman if he could have something engraved in the inside. "Can you engrave 'We will be together again…..I promise' on the inside?" he asked the salesmen. That was the saying that he always told Julie and Julie always told him, 'I will love you forever….I promise." With that accomplished, he put the ring in his safety deposit box at the bank.

He developed a scheme that he thought Julie would love that included the help of Andrew and Cassie. He had the chance to talk to the kids about his plan when Julie ran down to the grocery store to pick up some items they needed for lunch.

"Kids, you know that I love your mommy very much. We are going to surprise her! I need you to help me! We're gonna tell Mommy that we have a surprise for her. Remember how we surprised her at Christmas with her present? We'll sit her in the desk chair, ask her to close her eyes, and then we'll surprise her. I'll be hiding behind her. The two of you will be in front of her. When you say, "Open your eyes," you two will hand her a letter. She'll open the letter and will read it. Then at the bottom, it'll ask her to close her eyes and turn around. You know how that chair turns all the way around? When she turns around, you tell her to open her eyes. I'll be down on one knee and I'll open this little black box. There will be a really pretty ring in the box. That's the surprise!"

"Is that all she's getting? A little ring?" Andrew asked with some element of disappointment in his voice.

"Yes, Drewsy, but trust me, she'll love it," he explained as best he could calling Andrew by the nickname that had evolved naturally. "What do you think, Cassie?"

"Yeah! Yeah!" she said jumping and down. "A sa pwize! A sa pwize! For Mommy!"

Anthony realized that Andrew would have been more excited, if he gave Julie a play dump truck, but the ring would just have to do. Cassie would be just as excited if the ring were from a Cracker Jack box. She didn't know the difference.

"Ok, kids, let's practice!" Anthony said.
"Here's the chair. We're gonna to put it right here. OK? We'll sit Mommy here and ask her to keep her eyes closed." Cassie couldn't restrain her excitement and started jumping up and down

laughing. "OK, kids----listen Cassie----Andrew---
you're gonna give Mommy this envelope with this
letter when we tell her to open her eyes.
Remember---when we tell her to open her eyes, you
hand her this envelope. The letter will tell her to
close her eyes and turn around. You can help her
turn the chair around. I'm gonna to be right back
here like this," Anthony said as he got down on one
knee.

"Why, Daddy? Why do that?" Andrew managed to
say. He was puzzled as to why Daddy would kneel
down on the floor that way. It was new to him.

"It works this way, Drewsy. You'll see. Mommy
will like it," Jonathan tried to explain knowing they
had no clue what was really happening. He didn't
care---he just wanted them to do what they
rehearsed. He also knew that it had to be done very
soon, because the kids couldn't keep a secret for
any time at all. In fact, they better do it TODAY. In
fact, they better do it as soon as Julie gets home.
Otherwise, the kids are gonna forget what to do or
they're gonna tell their Mommy that they have a big
'sa pwize' for her.

They all looked out the front window until Julie's
car pulled into the driveway. The kids started
screaming at the top of their lungs. "Kid! Kids!
Calm down!" Anthony pleaded. "Act normal or
Mommy is gonna figure out what we're doing!"

130

Finally, they settled down, just in time for her to walk through the kitchen door. She put the groceries on the table and walked into the living room where the rest of the family was.

"Mommy?" Anthony said, "The kids and I have a surprise for you. You have to sit in this chair---right here." Cassis started giggling so hard that Andrew put his hand over her mouth as Anthony gave her the signal to be quiet.

With a very questioning look on her face, and a slight grin, Julie looked at Anthony and then sat in the chair as instructed.

Anthony and the kids yelled, "Close your eyes!" all at the same time. Cassis let out one final scream of excitement.

Julie closed her eyes and Anthony handed the kids the envelope with the letter. With a signal from Anthony, the kids asked her to open her eyes and they immediately handed her the envelope.

Julie opened the envelope, then pulled out the letter as she looked at both Andrew and Cassie with a smile. They were both staring at their mom with huge smiles on their faces. Julie had never seen them so excited! *What in the world is this?* she thought. *What is going on?* She really had no clue. As she pulled the letter out, the kids started jumping up and down and squealing. Anthony gave them the signal to settle down, but it was useless.

Julie read:

Dearest Julie,

I love you more than life itself. We were always meant to be together but were unknowingly kept apart for almost twenty-five years. But, now we are together and will be for the rest of our lives.

We have been blessed with two beautiful children who bring such love and joy to our lives every day.

We have been blessed to have the resources to get to spend every day together for the rest of our lives. Because of you, the sun shines brighter. Because of you, wine tastes sweeter. Because of you, the birds sing more sweetly.

I was given a new life on April many years ago when I received my kidney transplant. Now, I want to start another life with you.

Love,
Anthony

Julie, now close your eyes and turn your chair around.

Reading the last sentence, she looked up at the kids who are anxiously watching her every move. She started to figure everything out.

"Close your eyes! Close your eyes! The kids yelled. She closed her eyes. As she turned her chair around, the kids helped turn it.

"Open your eyes!" the kids screamed.

When Julie opened her eyes, she saw Anthony down on one knee and, of course, she knew what was happening then for sure. Her mouth opened wide in shock.

"Julie, will you marry me and make me the happiest man in the whole wide world?" Anthony asked.

Before Julie could answer, the kids both started jumping up and down yelling, "Yes! Yes!"

Julie and Anthony were laughing so hard that Anthony couldn't get up out of his one knee kneel and Julie couldn't answer Anthony's question.

The laughter finally subsided so Anthony asked one more time. "Julie, let me do a replay. Julie, will you marry me?"

"Of course, Anthony," she replied as Anthony took her into his arms. "I will marry you. I will always love you…..I promise."

The kids joined in on a group hug and then everyone started crying. The kids didn't really understand what all that meant but, because Anthony and Julie were crying, they cried, too.

The wedding was a very small family affair, quite unlike the million-dollar extravaganza called a wedding that Anthony and Marilyn had so many years ago. Julie's parents were there, of course, in addition to several other relatives from each side. There were some very close friends who were there and who were almost more excited than the bride and groom! Little Andrew and Cassie were the stars of the event.

The wedding was held in the backyard of a friend's house. It had a white, wood-carved gazebo and was just the right size for the wedding ceremony. Andrew and Cassie were dressed so nicely----he in a suit with bow tie; and she in a floor length, floral dress with a lace overlay. Cassie locked arms with Andrew and carried a little, white basket with pink rose petals. When they reached the front of the gazebo, they sprinkled the rose petals on the steps in preparation for the bride and groom.

When Anthony stood at the gazebo waiting for Julie to appear, he looked absolutely handsome. He was actually glowing from within. And then she appeared-----her eyes locked onto his. She wore a beautiful, long, lace-covered gown with long sleeves and round neckline. There was a carefully placed cluster of white flowers on one side of her head. She was radiant.

By now, everyone had heard the story of how the two had started out almost twenty-five years ago. That made the ceremony even that more emotional for everyone. Men and women alike were tearing up out of pure happiness for Anthony and Julie.

When Anthony compared the two weddings that he had been the groom in, he couldn't believe the difference. He knew Julie loved him more than anything in the world; he felt that Marilyn just loved "the moment." She wasn't really in love with him and he wasn't really in love with her. *I wonder how many men, or women, for that fact, go through the motion of a wedding, just because it is expected, perhaps thinking everything will work out. It doesn't matter anymore. I am here now, and this is right where I should be.*

The minister started the ceremony. He said the usual statements that he wanted to say before the vows were read. Julie and Anthony rewrote the usual vows to include Andrew and Cassi.

First, Anthony, led by the minister said, "I, Anthony, take thee Julie, to be my wedded wife, to have and to hold, from this day forward, for better, for worse, for richer, for poorer, in sickness and in health, to love and to cherish, till death do us part, according to God's holy ordinance and thereto, I pledge thee my faith."

Julie repeated the same vow. "I, Julie, take thee Anthony, to be my wedded husband, to have and to hold, from this day forward, for better, for worse, for richer, for poorer, in sickness and in health, to love and to cherish, till death do us part, according to God's holy ordinance and thereto, I pledge thee my faith."

Then it was time for the children to be included with their own vows. Led by the minister and with only a couple of words at a time, they said, "We, Andrew and Cassie, ……take you Daddy,…… to be our father…. from this day forward,…. for better or worse,…. in sickness and in health,…. and to love you…..forever and forever." The kids were very serious and said their vows very well. They didn't pronounce all of the words accurately, but that's what made it more meaningful. The friends and family members were crying. They couldn't help it.

Then it was time for the ring ceremony. As Anthony placed the ring on Julie's finger, he said, "Julie, I give you this ring as a sign of my commitment and the desire of my heart. May it always be a reminder that I have chosen you above all others, and from this day forward, we shall be united as husband and wife." Anthony slid the ring onto her finger.

Julie repeated the vows to Anthony as she placed the ring on his finger.

Anthony and Julie turned to Andrew and Cassie and said the following vows: "Andrew and Cassie, we give you these rings to show you our love and commitment as parents. We will love and care for you for the rest of our lives." Anthony placed a small ring on Andrew's finger as Julie placed a small ring on Cassie's finger. Then they all hugged.

Then the minister said, "Anthony, you may kiss the bride."

When the preacher asked Anthony to kiss the bride, the children giggled. Anthony held Julie closely and gave her the most amazing kiss. With that, he was telling her that he loved her more than anything in the world and that he would always be there for her. *We will be together again.....I promise.*

Chapter 18
Moving to a New House

The Adkins family lived in Julie's small two-bedroom home until they felt it was the right time to move. It was a difficult decision, at first, because the little house brought so much closeness to the family. But as the kids grew older, it was decided that each could use their own bedroom and bathroom. Besides, Anthony and Julie wanted to give the kids more room to run and play. They also wanted them to have room to have friends over for sleep-overs if they wanted.

Anthony and Julie discussed what kind of house they would be looking for. She preferred a one-story home, opting to keep the kids closer to the master bedroom. In the back of her mind, she remembered the fire that took *their* son's life. That fire was in a two-story house. She never mentioned that to Anthony, but he somehow sensed it.

"I'd love a place near the edge of town," Julie said with an element of excitement in her voice. "I've always wanted the children to have a miniature horse and maybe some other animals like a miniature goat or cow! Those minis are just sooo cute!"

"Whom did you say you wanted animals for?" Anthony said with a smile on his face. "Did you say for the children?" He knew very well that Julie loved animals and she was just using the children as an excuse. He knew her so well."

"OK, well, you are probably right. I have always wanted a mini. What do you think?" she answered.

"Well, let's keep that in mind, because you can't keep farm animals just anywhere." He had an idea, but he wasn't going to tell Julie about it.

While Julie was busy working on a project for the kid's school, Anthony started scouting out potential houses. His real estate buddy knew right what Anthony was looking for. He thought a few adjustments and additions might have to be made, but other than that, the new place might be just what would work.

When Anthony's buddy, Arnold, showed him the house at the edge of town, he immediately liked it. It was a beautiful home with fantastic drive up appeal. Sitting on the edge of town, the house had five acres of land attached and was very private, nestled away from the surrounding houses. The backyard had a beautiful pool and plenty of space for a small barn and an animal pen. It also had space for a koi pond. The two men went inside to check out the interior. It was immaculate and was certainly move-in ready.

"Arnold, this is just what I think Julie would like. It is a one-story house, so we'll still be together on one floor, and the house is simply beautiful. I want to have a small barn built beyond the pool with a white fence for the animals," Anthony said.

"Oh, I didn't know y'all had any animals!" Arnold exclaimed.

"We don't right now, but I can bet ya a pair of boots that we're going to!" Anthony laughed. "So, we better get someone building on that right away!"

"Will do---I know just the right person," Arnold offered.

"And while you're at it, let's have your guy build a koi pond over there by that beautiful magnolia tree." Now Arnold is looking at him kind of funny. "You know---koi---large goldfish?" Anthony said.

"Oh, sure. I know---I know," Arnold answered. The men laughed.

2

It was all Anthony could do to keep his project a secret. He wanted to tell Julie about it, but he didn't. Wrestling back and forth on the subject, he finally decided to keep the whole thing a secret and then surprise her and the kids when everything was ready. He knew Julie extremely well, but if for some reason, she didn't like the house, he could sell it, and they could find another.

Then he had another idea. Julie said she wanted a miniature horse and perhaps a miniature goat or two. *Why don't I buy some animals and have them here when Julie and the kids see the place for the first time? Won't that be exciting? Of course, if Julie decides against the place, we will have to house the animals in our backyard with the hamburger grill and the lawn furniture, but maybe that won't be too bad*, he thought to himself as he chuckled.

After a just a month, the house, the mini barn, and the koi pond were ready. He inspected it and was very pleased. He drove a distance to a farm store and was pleased that so many farm animals were there to be selected. The miniature horse was easy. There was one that was very tiny. He was jet black and already had a long mane. Anthony bought him.

Then he looked at some miniature pot belly pigs but also saw what they looked like once they grew up. He decided against that selection. The piglets were so precious, but mommy and daddy potbelly weren't. *I think I'll pass on those. Julie never said anything about pigs.*

Moving on to the miniature goats, Anthony learned that they were called African Pygmy Goats. They would never be larger than a small dog and were very compatible with the horse. Goats and horses get along with each other very well. The first goat Anthony saw was a light-gray color with black markings. It looked very exotic. It was so small that one could easily hold it. Turns out it was a female named Annabell.

"Now, ya don't have to keep the name if ya buy her, but we're all family 'round here and we name 'um as soon as they're born," the store manager said.

The other goat was the same size and was solid white. He even had white hooves. He was precious.

"What's his name?" Anthony asked.

"Well, we call him Billy. That's short for Billy Goat. Get it?" the manager replied with a chuckle.

"Yeah, I get it---I get it. I just can't decide on which one to get," Anthony answered somewhat confused.

"Well, let me help ya out with that problem. One customer just bought one goat to keep her mini horse company. As the goat grew up, he wanted to butt heads with the horse. All goats butt heads---it's just what they do for fun, I guess. Long story short---the horse wasn't keen on butting heads. He didn't like it one bit. So, the customer ends up buying two goats so they can butt heads all day long if they want. Then they lived happily ever after. Get it?"

"I get it," Anthony said with a sigh. "OK, I'll buy them both. You're a good salesman." Anthony shook the man's hand.

142

"Can I hep ya with anything else?" the manager said. "Of course, I'll load ya up with the feed they're gonna need and the supplies---ya know--- combs, brushes, hoof picks---fly shampoo---"

"Oh wow---this project is getting a little out of control! Am I sure I want to do this?" Anthony kidded as he took out his wallet.

"I'm sure you're sure," the man joked. "And you'll know it later when ya show the animals to your wife."

With that, Anthony arranged for the animals to be delivered to the "mini ranch" that he was now calling it. He wanted everything to be in place for the big reveal. He could picture the animals in their little pen---white rail fencing---and the mini barn---- red and white. Juli*e's gonna love this!*

After lunch that Saturday, Anthony piled the kids into the car and told Julie that he wanted to show her a potential house. They drove to the edge of town and to the winding entrance that led to the house. Trees lined the driveway, but the house couldn't be seen because of the curves in the road. Then, around the last curve, the house could be seen standing picturesque against the green pastures.

"Is that it?" Julie exclaimed as they pulled up to the front. "It's gorgeous! Oh, my! Can we go in?" Everyone started bailing out of the car.

"Sure, Arnold parked around the back I'm sure, but he's here to let us in. He's probably already inside."

Everyone loved the house. The kids were so excited they were squealing. Julie loved everything about the inside, but she hadn't even seen the backyard, yet. Then Arnold led them through the backdoor.

"A pool! A pool!" the kids yelled. They had never really talked about getting a house with a pool much, but it was obvious that a pool would be a great selling point for the kids. Then Julie saw the mini barn. When the animals heard the talking and excitement, they came out from behind the barn as if on cue. *Boy, this couldn't be better if I had rehearsed it with them!* Anthony thought.

Julie's mouth was wide open with shock. "Oh, my goodness! Look at those precious animals! Anthony, do these animals belong to the owners of the house? Would we be able to buy them?"

"No, Julie, you can't buy them," Anthony said then added, "Because I've already bought them. They are yours." Julie screamed then swung her arms around Anthony, hugging him tightly. "My dream come true!"

"I thought *I* was your dream come true!" he said laughing and trying to get out of her bear hug. "Do I have to compete with a mini horse and two African

Pygmy goats for affection? I should have thought this idea out more thoroughly."

The kids had already run over to the fence and were peering through the railing, calling the animals. "Here, pony, pony. Here little goat," the kids called out.

By now, Anthony and Julie had caught up with the kids. "Kids, the mini horse is named Bo. That's short for Beaujolais, but that is a red wine, so I thought his real name would be Beaujo*neigh* since horses 'neigh.' Do you get it?" Of course, Julie got it right away and thought it was the funniest thing she had ever heard. The kids only looked at him with blank looks on their faces. "Ok, forget all that----his name is Bo." Everyone laughed.

"What about the goats! What about the goats!" the kids yelled pointing to the goats. One goat was a light gray color with black markings on its feet, legs, face, and down the center of its back. It was very exotic looking like those antelopes in Africa. The other goat was solid white with white hooves.

"Well, the gray one is a girl and her name is Annabell. The white one is a boy and his name is Billy," Anthony said deciding to forgo the explanation of Billy Goat. "We can change their names if you want, but this is what the farm store named them when they were born." Julie caught the "Billy Goat" anyway and died laughing.

"Annabell and Billy," Julie said. "I like those names. Let's keep 'um."

With all of the excitement of the farm animals, no one even noticed the koi pond, until Anthony asked them to take a walk over to the magnolia tree. Once the kids saw it, they ran full force. It was a rather large koi pond, built with a natural configuration and a waterfall on one end. The kids peered into the pond and saw a very large, solid orange goldfish. It was almost fourteen inches long.

"Look Mommy! Look Daddy! A goldfish!" the kids yelled. Julie and Anthony looked at each other, absorbing the excitement of the children.

"Well, Julie----what do you think? It's your decision on whether we get keep house or not. We can look for another one if you want," Anthony offered that option.

"Are you kidding me?" she exclaimed. "Anthony, you knew exactly what I have always dreamed of. If I had written down everything I have ever wanted, it would be this place. You're not taking this away from me---ever." He knew she loved it. And she did.

3

The family couldn't wait to move in. After they got settled, they added several rabbits to the mix. Then Anthony came home one day with some baby Mallard ducks. They were so tiny when they were young that Anthony had to make a ramp leading up to the top of the plastic baby pool so that they could swim around in the water. As they grew, they didn't need the ramp. Several white ducks were added also and in no time at all, the yard was filled with rabbits running around wild, ducks swimming in baby pools and numerous cats and dogs joining in on the fray.

"It's true about rabbits," Anthony mentioned to Julie one morning when they were getting ready to start their day.

"What do you mean?" she asked really not knowing what he was going to say.

"They multiply----like rabbits!" he answered knowing that they now had around sixteen rabbits. They were having large 50-pound bags of Purina Rabbit Chow and 50-pound bags of Horse Chow delivered every two weeks. When they ordered the goat chow, they found that the goats preferred to eat horse chow so they let them.

One day the children ran into the house totally out of breath. "Mommy, Daddy! Come quick! Bo's mouth is bleeding! Something's wrong!"

Anthony and Julie ran out to the pen where Bo was standing. Anthony opened Bo's mouth where he saw the blood. "Kids, it's OK. Bo just lost a tooth. You know how your baby tooth bled a little when we pulled it out? Well, Bo must have lost his baby tooth. No worries. He's going to be OK." It was times like these that life interesting.

What the family didn't know at that time was the fact that goats *love* to butt heads with each other. The first time the kids saw the two goats butting heads, they thought the goats were fighting. Andrew ran into the house screaming for his daddy to come see the goats. "Daddy! They're fighting! The goats are fighting! Come look!" Anthony ran out the door and to the animal yard.

"Drewsy, they're not fighting. They're actually playing. They have fun doing that!" Anthony said trying to convince Andrew and Cassie that the goats would be fine.

On another day, the family saw the goats standing on Bo's back. How cute! At first Bo didn't seem to mind or maybe he didn't *know* what to think about it. After a while, he got irritated with their antics and wouldn't let them stand on his back any more. Knowing goats like to climb up on things-----just ask Bo----Anthony built them a tower of bales of hay so they could climb anytime they wanted. Animals can be quite interesting.

In addition to having all of their own rabbits, when anyone in the neighborhood found a domesticated bunny, they assumed it belonged to the family with the mini farm. They would bring the bunny with them to the front door and usually say, "I think I found one of your rabbits."

Julie would always say, "Well, I don't think this one is ours, but we'll be happy to take it from you. It can join the others." The people always acted so grateful because most of them had no way of caring for a rabbit.

One day, Betty, a teacher friend of Julie, asked her if she would want to adopt a dog. He was a very pretty, well-groomed schnauzer. He was light gray with dark black markings. Betty could never bring herself to cropping his ears so he had floppy ears that sometimes stood up like a donkey.

Betty hated to give him up----he had almost been like a child to her---but at the same time, he was driving her and her husband crazy. When she arrived at home after a full day of teaching, he jumped all over her. He was so happy that she was at home! He had been in an empty house all day long, and he couldn't wait for the humans to come home. If she or her husband tried to do gardening in the backyard, he jumped all over them. If they left him in the house, he barked excessively. They loved him but just couldn't handle him any longer. Then came the straw that broke the camel's back. When Betty got home from school one day, she found that "Randolph" had chewed the skirt off one of her favorite chairs. It was totally ruined. It couldn't be repaired.

Of course, Julie agreed to take him. The family already had a female Doberman in addition to a cat in the house, but everyone agreed to taking on the mischievous schnauzer.

On the day that Betty handed Randolph, over to Julie, Betty also gave her his bed, his favorite blanket, several chewy toys, a package of rawhide chews, and a folder chronicling his medical records. Every veterinarian visit was neatly on a ledger---date---time---reason for visit----prognosis---fee. *Wow,* Julie thought. *Betty really treated this dog like a human being. Most parents don't keep records like this for their own children!*

Betty cried when she handed Randolph over. Julie tried to assure her that he would be fine. "I think he will like it at our house. He will have plenty of other animals to keep him busy. We will love him." Julie didn't want to stay any longer then needed, because she could tell Betty was very sad. Maybe getting Randolph out of her sight would help a little. She drove off.

Julie was right. All of the stories Betty told her about Randolph just didn't hold true in the Adkins household. Randolph was so busy running around and around with the Doberman and the cat that by the end of the day, his tongue was hanging out with exhaustion. He didn't even look up at the end of the day. But he seemed like one happy puppy.

4

Once, when Annabel the goat needed a vet visit, the family put her in the small pet carrier in the back seat of the car, between Cassie and Andrew and took off. When Anthony drove around the corner a little too fast, he cried out, "Hang on, Annabell!"

That statement, "Hang on, Annabell!" became the thing everyone said when a road got too bumpy, or the car went around a curve too fast. Even when Annabell wasn't in the car, which she really never was, they *still* said it. Even when riding their tricycles and bicycles, if the ride got bumpy, the kids would yell, "Hang on, Annabell!"

Many years later, when someone took a turn a little too fast, or even if the hay ride got too bumpy---any time things got jumbled, someone would call out, "Hold on Annabell!"

Chapter 19
The Children Grow Up

Moving out to the mini farm was one of the best
things the family ever did. Everyone loved playing
with the animals, but they also learned about
responsibility. They had to feed and groom the
animals and take care of them when they were sick.
They learned that even if it were really cold outside,
they had to feed the animals and make sure they had
clean water.

They enjoyed watching and feeding the koi and
soon had several other koi to add to the pond. They
learned how to clean the filters and maintain the
pump that controlled the waterfall. The koi were
trained to eat out of their hands and would actually
swim over to the edge of the pond to greet the
children.

The children learned the lesson of taking care of
what they had, both inside the house and in the
backyard. They didn't take anything for granted.
Anthony and Julie taught them well.

Anthony enrolled Andrew on a T-Ball team when
he was just turning five. He could hit the ball pretty
far and he could run pretty fast. On one particular
day, Andrew hit the ball but got confused to which
direction he was supposed to run. Immediately upon
hitting the ball, the crowd yelled, "Run, Andrew!
Run!" But seeing that he was running the wrong
way, they yelled, "The other way! The other way!"

Anthony nearly fell out of the bleachers laughing. *Priceless! Priceless! This will give us laughs for years!*

Andrew graduated Tee-Ball for the Little League. He never had a problem with which direction to run again, but the family never let him forget it. It was a topic brought up frequently, even with visitors. He thought it was funny, too, and it gave him a good laugh. The family always went to his games and supported the entire team. The team had a chance to play in a fancy tournament in the adjacent town, but they didn't have any uniforms. The team parents discussed the idea of having bake sales and car washing events, but it was still going to take more ideas to produce the money needed for all of the uniforms. It was a no-brainer. Anthony announced at the next parent meeting that an anonymous donor had donated enough money to buy all of the uniforms without the bake sales and the car washes.

"I found this envelope in my mailbox," was all Anthony said making it seem like he was as surprised as anyone. The truth was, he *did* find that particular envelope in his mailbox. He was not lying. It just didn't have the money in it. Anthony put the money in it. I'm sure most of the parents actually believed Anthony had done it, but they didn't question.

When Cassie went to kindergarten, she was so proud of her big brother who was a year ahead. She looked up to him and thought he was soooo smart. Once when she was being tested by the counselor at school, she showed that she really looked up to her brother. When asked one question that she didn't know the answer to, Cassie replied, "I don't know, but my brother knows. Do you want me to go ask him? He's next door." The counselor fought to hold back laughter. It was one of the funniest answers she had ever heard.

Another one of Cassie's answers resulted in the counselor actually writing it down. She really didn't want to ever forget this one. The counselor asked Cassie, "Cassie, how many inches are in a foot?" Cassie leaned over and measured her foot with her little fingers. She held up her two index fingers to show the length of her foot and said, "This many."

A third funny answer was recorded. When asked, "What does the word migrate mean?" Cassie answered, "My great aunt?"

Cassie loved dancing. She took tap, ballet, and jazz lessons at Catherine's School of Dance studio. Recitals were held once a year and the parents had to come up with the costumes designed by the head instructor. Julie could sew so that is what she did. One costume for the song, "Singing in the Rain" entailed buying an umbrella, covering it with silver satin, and gluing blue raindrops all over it. The short dance skirt and top were made to match. Over the months, many pairs of tennis shoes were covered with sequins or sparkly fabric glued on like the factory had done it.

Cassie also took piano lessons and later baton twirling lessons. Jonathan and Julie were constantly in motion taking the kids from one lesson or activity to the other, but they always made time to gather around the dinner table at night and discuss the day.

3

When the state fair was coming to a neighboring town, Julie and Anthony decided to take the children. It would be a great family activity and one to be remembered for many years to come. The kids didn't know what to expect.

The family arrived at the fairgrounds but had to park far from the main gate. There were so many people! Once inside the gate, Julie took Cassie's hand and Anthony took Andrew's hand. "Kids, let's stay together----it's so easy to get separated and lost!" Anthony advised.

The kids' eyes were wide open when they saw the huge Ferris wheel and the roller coaster. They had never seen anything like it. Everywhere they looked, they saw children riding on exciting rides and screaming at the top of their lungs. They saw some rides that looked so scary, that they would never get on them no matter what! Julie and Anthony decided to try the merry-go-round first. The kids jumped on the large, colorful horses while their parents stood alongside. Both kids thought it was the greatest ride. In fact, they ended up riding it four more times!

As the family walked through the food court, they took in the wonderful smells of hot dogs, hamburgers, French fries, corn on the cob, corny dogs, turkey legs, and funnel cakes. While Julie and Cassie squirted mustard on their corny dogs, Anthony and Andrew each tried their hand at footlong hotdogs. When they finished the corny dogs and hotdogs, the family had to try the funnel cakes and caramel apples. Cassie and Andrew thought they were in heaven. Although Julie always tried to control their sugar intake, the state fair was different. This was a time to eat whatever they wanted. And they did!

The kids had never seen the various booths luring unsuspecting participants to try their hands at throwing darts, shooting basketball, or throwing rings on coke bottles. Julie and Anthony wanted the kids to experience the fun. They had a great time and each won a little consolation prize of a tiny stuffed animal. If you play several games and win nothing, you get a small consolation prize. As Anthony told Julie later with laughter, "Those little stuffed animals only cost us $37 dollars each!"

At daylight turned to night time, there was even more excitement. The lights were fantastic and there were so many sights that the kids didn't know which way to look. They were mesmerized. Anthony and Julie got their enjoyment out of just watching the kids.

Going to the petting zoo was particularly fun for the kids-----and Julie. They saw a baby kangaroo, baby pot belly pigs, several baby goats, and even a baby giraffe. They had never seen a giraffe before! There were several other exotic animals like African antelopes and large turtles. They enjoyed the llamas and baby zebra. Anthony looked over at Julie and knew what was going through her head: *If only I could figure out a way to get a baby zebra or baby giraffe and actually keep them at home!* He imagined that she was thinking that.

Just as he thought that himself, Andrew said, "Daddy, can't we get a baby zebra? Couldn't he stay in the pen with Bo?

"I'd love to have one, Drewsy, but I think there is a lot more involved in having exotic animals. I don't think just anyone can go buy a zebra. Let's just stick to what we have and take care of them, OK?" Anthony explained.

After a few more rides and more food, it was time to get the children home. They had seen everything they could see and just about ate everything that could be eaten. Once they reached their car, the

kids jumped in the backseat and were asleep within
five minutes.

4

Christmas in the Adkins' household was very
special. Julie made a point to decorate most of the
house, especially their family room. The family put
up a tall tree in the corner of the room with white
twinkling lights. A collection of ornaments started
by Julie while still in high school were carefully
placed on the tree, but new ones were added each
year. The kids loved picking out colorful
ornaments at the local stores. Cassie always wanted
to pick up ornaments with flowers and animals on
them. Alek liked the ones that were stars or
different shapes. Anthony had to show the children
how to place the icicles one-by-one on the tree
branches. After they got tired, they wanted to throw
them in bunches. Then Julie had to pull icicles from
the bunches and place them where they were
needed. It was certainly a family affair.

One of the traditions that Julie wanted to establish
with the children just like she had done with Alek
was Christmas cookie decorating. She made sugar
cookie dough and let the kids use cookie cutters to
cut out the cookies in shapes like Christmas trees,
ornaments, stars, Santas, and presents. The kids
loved making the cookie shapes. Sometimes they
wanted to taste the raw cookie dough but Julie felt

that was fine. In fact, that is what she did when her mother made sugar cookies also!

Then they baked the cookies. The smell of cookies baking filled the kitchen. The kids were very anxious for the cookies to come out of the oven. They couldn't help but eat some of the hot cookies. Hot cookies and milk? How great is that! Anthony ate about three cookies before Julie yelled, "Hey guys! There won't be any cookies left to decorate if you eat them all! How sad would that be!"

Actually, Julie knew that eating hot cookies was an important part of the Christmas Decorating Event. She planned ahead and made plenty of cookies to decorate and save for others.

Julie made sure that she had plenty of colored icing and all the sprinkles and decorations that would make the cookies beautiful. Even Anthony got in on the fun. He took a Christmas tree, covered it with green icing, and then placed little, candy, silver balls on each limb of the tree. Then he put a few red sprinkles to form ornaments. He was so proud of his little Christmas tree cookie. As time went on and the kids grew older, they made prettier and prettier Christmas cookies.

"Wouldn't it be great to decorate cookies and take them to the Senior Living Center?" Anthony asked when the family decorated cookies at the kitchen table.

"Yes! Cassie and Andrew both thought it would be a great idea. Then they tried even harder knowing their cookies would be given as gifts to the seniors at the retirement community. Julie suggested they wrap them in cellophane and tie a little red bow on each one. It became a tradition in the Adkins household. Every year after that, even after Andrew went off to college, the entire family gathered in the kitchen and made Christmas cookies.

Julie loved poinsettias and was skilled at keeping them alive. The large pot on either side of the fireplace was watered and protected so that, after winter when the weather warmed up, she could put them out on the patio. The red leaves turned to green and then she had a beautiful, full, green plant. If she followed the directions on how to make them turn red again for Christmas, she would have beautiful red leaves once again.

There were several red candles strategically placed as decoration and they also had a collection of Santas and nutcrackers. The kids were thrilled when their parents pulled the decorations out of storage. It was almost like they were seeing the items for the first time each Christmas!

"Oh! Look at this one!" Alek exclaimed as he pulled a small Santa from the box. "I forgot about this one!"

Cassie pulled everything she could reach from one box and then would go to the next box. "I love this! I love this!"

5

One of the other traditions Julie started for the kids was decorating Styrofoam balls to make Christmas decorations. She bought several white styrofoam balls, several rolls of velvet and satin ribbon, beads of all colors, and straight pins. Julie showed the children how to take the ribbon, put a pin on one end to hold it to the ball, and then wrap it around the ball to secure on the other side. Then she placed individual beads on the ribbon or the ball with straight pins. Sometimes she bought costume jewelry to get colored beads. The kids showed their creativity with different ideas for the balls. One ball was covered with red velvet ribbon, had bright red beads going down the middle of each ribbon, and red sequins down each side of each ribbon. It took a long time to decorate, but it was beautiful.

Every year, the family attended the Christmas program at their church on Christmas Eve and then headed to Julie's parents' home to have dinner. While there, they opened presents that her parents had for them. By miracle, every time they arrived to their own home, Santa had already come and toys were around the tree. Once, when they arrived home, and were sitting around unwrapping presents, the front door opened. A large red wagon rolled through the front door and "Santa" said, "Ho, ho, ho!" Then the door shut. Alek and Cassie stared at the door. Their mouths dropped open. They were in a state of shock! Santa had *just* come to their house!! They were totally silent until it sunk in. Then the screaming began. They ran to the wagon and started pulling out all of the toys Santa had left for them. Santa knew just what they wanted. It was a miracle.

After the holiday season, it was time to put all of the decorations back in the garage and attic. The kids felt it was a little sad, but their parents were ready for the Santas and the candles and the tree to be put away.

6

Christmas was the family's favorite time of the year, but a good second favorite was any day of the week that it snowed! Every winter there was at least one great snowfall. The children started screaming when they looked outside and saw the white, winter wonderland that waited for them. They bundled up in their warmest winter coats, winter mittens, and furry leather boots. Anthony and Julie had to hurry to get their coats on to catch up with the kids. Running outside, the kids immediately made snowballs to throw at each other. Soon, Julie and Anthony were throwing snowballs themselves. Giggling and laughing, snowballs were flying in all directions. Then, the kids ran to the other side of the house where there was a slope that was perfect for sledding down on plastic garbage can lids. "Weeee! Weeee!" the kids exclaimed as they slid past their parents sometimes twirling all the way around.

"They couldn't have more fun even if we bought them expensive sleds. Right, Mom?" Anthony yelled out. "Right, Dad!" Julie yelled back.

After the kids got their fill of sledding down the slope, they settled in to make a snowman. "Come on Mommy! Come Daddy! Help us build a snowman!" They started rolling snow to make the bottom of the snowman. They could only roll it so far, before their parents had to take over. Then came the middle ball for the snowman's upper body. Meanwhile, Julie ran into the house and grabbed a carrot, an old hat, and a worn scarf. On the way out of the back door, she picked up the bag of charcoal briquettes used for grilling. She got back just in time to finish up the snowman. When she pulled out the items, the kids screamed at the top of their lungs. The hat went on the snowman's head and Julie tied the scarf around the neck just under the head.

"No, no! The carrot is not for the mouth. It's for his nose!" Julie yelled as she grabbed the carrot from Andrew's mitten and placed it where the nose should be. Handing the kids the charcoal pieces, she watched as they made the snowman's eyes and buttons. They added small walnuts still in the shells for the mouth.

163

"Why, that is just about the greatest snowman I've ever seen!" Anthony declared while being truly amazed at the final result. "It really does look like the snowmen you see in the picture books." *Amazing!*

After a playful morning out in the snow, the whole crew decided to head back to the warmth of the house. Peeling off coats, boots, and mittens, the kids ran to stand in front of the fireplace where their father had made a wonderful fire. Meanwhile, Julie made hot chocolate and put out a plate of small sandwiches. She knew the kids would be starving.

After they ate, took hot baths, and put on their pajamas, Julie surprised them with 'snow ice cream.' The kids had never had snow ice cream before. Then Julie found out that Anthony had never had it, either! What a treat!

"Now, how do you make this?" Anthony asked as he tasted the sweet, cold ice cream.

"Just get a bowl of snow---really clean snow---then stir in a little sugar and vanilla. See? It's easy," she said.

Anthony walked up to Julie, put his arms around her and said, "Life is good."

The kids grew up quickly. Soon, they were in middle school and were still actively involved in extra-curricular activities. Cassie started middle school basketball and loved it. By the beginning of high school, she dropped piano lessons and twirling lessons because she was too busy. Cassie played basketball, volleyball, tennis, and ran track. She became a high school majorette that allowed her to be in the marching band and twirl on the sidelines of all of the football games. She loved it. It was so interesting that Cassie followed in Julie's footsteps.

Andrew began playing golf while in middle school and did very well. While playing in his very first tournament in ninth grade, Andrew was the player leading the pack. Adults were following him on the course. One man in particular told him, "Andrew, see that tree just on the side of the fairway? Well, if you aim directly at it, you will miss it and it won't cause you a problem. Andrew aimed right at the tree and his shot hit it dead on! He ended up in second place instead of first place because of that shot.

When the kids hit the high school level, the two had problems with each other. Andrew was always late. Cassie was always late, because she had to wait for Andrew to drive them to school. Cassie was a majorette, so she was required to be at the very front of the band when marching at half time. Every morning of the week when the entire marching band practiced the marching routine for the football games, Andrew and Cassie were late. Everyone else was standing there on the football field ready to practice the routine when Cassie had to run out to stand at the front of the band. Every eye was on her, or at least she thought everyone was looking at her. She was so embarrassed. Andrew, on the other hand, played the tuba, so he could just show up at the very back of the band and no one even noticed him. Cassie was humiliated. First of all, she was never late to anything ever! Now, her dear brother was making her late every day!

Even when the band wasn't practicing marching but was just practicing in the band hall, Cassie had to walk in late, go to the instrument room, open the French horn case, and then step over and around everyone to get to the middle of the band. Andrew could walk to the very back of the band hall and sit at the tuba that was already ready for him. No problem for him.

When Cassie couldn't take it any longer, she changed the clocks in the house to show that they were later than actual time. So, when the clock said it was 7:45 am, it was really 7:30 am. That trick worked for exactly two days. They were on time for two times during the whole school year. Cassie was happy. Somehow, Andrew figured it out and that was the end of that. Probably, he saw that they were actually on time twice in a row, so he started investigating it. One look at the clock showed it was fifteen minutes off.

It wasn't until Andrew went off to college that Cassie didn't have to share a car and was finally able to get to school on time.

Chapter 20
The Empty Nest Syndrome

Over time, the kids grew up, went off to college, married, and had children of their own. Julie and Anthony were faced with the 'empty nest' syndrome. They never had difficulty with having an empty nest. Actually, it was Julie's second empty nest. First, Alek grew up and went away to college and then married. Now, his kids---her other children---were leaving them with an empty nest. They were so glad to have finally found each other again, that they lived in a type of permanent happiness.

One evening as they were talking, both Anthony and Julie remembered all the times that pennies appeared in one or the other's belongings---on purpose, of course.

"Anthony, do you remember the time I had pennies delivered to your room when you were in Denver on that business trip for your father?" she asked.

"Yes, I remember being blown away by that. I was already in love with you, but that really did it. Do you remember the time I placed the penny under your napkin when we were having dinner at the restaurant? That was a surprise, wasn't it?" he said.

"Yes, I'd always been the one planting pennies and then you did, so it was a surprise. Remember the windshield wiper penny? Julie said with a twinkle in her eye. She always thought that was one of the best 'penny placements' that she had done."

"You won the prize for that one. How about when I put the penny on your bathroom mirror, when I had to go out of town? I carefully put the tape on the back so you couldn't see what was holding it to the mirror," Anthony said quite proud of himself.

"Do you remember the time I taped a penny on the receiver of the phone so that when you answered the phone you would see it? Anthony asked.

"And the one on the car seat….and the one on the top of the beer can….and the one on your pillow when I was gone over night," Julie mentioned not knowing if he would really remember all of those times.

"I remember each and every one of those," he answered without hesitation. "Funny how each of those incidents seem so small, but they were really so gigantic----and we can remember them from all of those years ago. Amazing."

They continued remembering penny incidents until it got too late to stay awake. Along the way, many years ago, they changed the meaning from 'I am thinking about you.' to 'I love you.' It just seemed more appropriate.

Anthony kept each and every penny that Julie had planted for him. For quite some time, he collected them on the bottom of one of his drawers. Once a penny was placed in the drawer, it was never removed. The pennies were representative of many wonderful memories.

"Hey---Jules----I have to ask you something. Remember when I tracked you down after you moved to Connecticut? Do you remember when I met you in your house with the red door?" he asked.

She wondered where he was going with the conversation. "Yes, I remember that day very well. I opened my door and you appeared. I just stared at you at first, because I didn't believe what I was seeing. You came in and we both didn't know what to think----I think."

"Yes, when you said you weren't married, I remember asking you if you were still in love with Alek's father. When you said, "Yes," my heart fell. I actually thought that you had gone through a divorce but was still in love with the father of your child. Thinking back, I noticed that you didn't really tell me anything else to clarify the situation. Why were you so evasive?" he questioned.

"Don't you remember? I thought you were still married--- at first. So, I didn't want to say or do anything that would take the focus away from your marriage. I couldn't do that. Then, you told me you were no longer married and hadn't been for over four years. That opened everything up for me.

170

Don't you remember that is when I asked you to walk with me?"

"Yes, we walked to the cemetery and you showed me Alek's headstone. I was so confused! The first thing I noticed was his last name. I actually thought you married someone with Johnson as a last name. It wasn't until I saw his birthdate that I started figuring. Why did you wait for me to try to figure it out?" he questioned.

"Darling, I don't know why I did what I did. You have to remember that I was in total shock when you appeared at my door. I probably wasn't thinking at all. Then, I could have told you right there in my living room, but maybe I needed time to think through *how* to tell you. Maybe the walk to the cemetery was the time I needed. Maybe I needed to see your reaction. I don't know. I really don't. I also didn't know if you would get angry for not telling you in the first place. I just know that once you knew that Alek was your own son, and you reacted the way you did, I knew everything was going to be fine. You held me in your arms and we cried. Our lives were cleansed with our crying. You held me all the way back to my house." She explained.

"I held you all the way back to the house because there was no way I was ever going to let you out of my sight again," he said holding her tightly.

"Anthony, if you had not searched and found me, we would not have had the wonderful life we have had. The children would not have had the wonderful father that you have been to them; I would not have been happy like I have been since you've come into my life. I have so much to thank you for," she said sincerely.

Chapter 21
Volunteering and Philanthropy

Having the kids out of the house meant they had much more time to work on other projects. Anthony suggested that he and Julie start volunteering their time and money. She agreed.

One night, Anthony and Julie sat around talking about what kind of volunteering they would be able to do, and also how they would be able to help others financially. Anthony was extremely wealthy, and his wealth was growing more and more each year. He made sure that trust funds were put into place to take care of Andrew and Cassie and any children and grandchildren that they would have. He wanted the trust to be handled securely and efficiently, so that the funds would grow over time but be handled where many generations of the Adkins family tree would reap the benefits of Anthony's financial expertise. He wanted the trust funds to supplement income, not supplant income. He knew too many people who were ruined by being given too much---by making life too easy with no work. He didn't want that to happen to any of the recipients because of the money they were going to inherit.

2

One of the stories Anthony told Julie about concerned his second cousin. His cousin was born to hardworking parents who owned a large ranch in

Texas. They tried to have children but experienced a failed pregnancy every time. There were several miscarriages. Finally, they had a child-----Bill. Every summer, when his father needed help with the ranch, Anthony and several other teenagers and guys in their early twenties were hired. The work was hard. It was hot and windy and the work was dirty. The 'cowboys' worked hard all morning and then they were fed a good lunch before heading back out to the fields. Bill always went out with the cowboys in the morning but never went back out after lunch. He was "sick" or "had a headache" or "his leg hurt." There was always an excuse. He just didn't want to work, and his father let him get by with it.

When it was time for Bill to go to college, he went off to a school that he never had to pay for himself. He hadn't learned how to work, so he couldn't do the school work, either. He flunked out.

Bill convinced his mother and father that if they would just buy him a liquor store, that he would be able to run it and that would be his life's work. They bought a liquor store for him. He ran it into the ground and lost everything.

He tried several other things, but nothing ever worked. He knew he never HAD to be successful because he knew his parents would bail him out---- and they did.

174

His parents grew old and were in poor health. When they passed away, he inherited the ranch. It was a sprawling working cattle ranch that was quite successful. Instead of keeping the ranch that would have been a good income for the rest of his life, Bill sold the ranch and financed the sale. The buyer agreed to pay a certain amount each month for thirty years. Just like a house mortgage. Bill had thirty years of payments to look forward to. He lived fairly frugally, renting a small house in town. He never worked. At the end of thirty years, Bill was only in his sixties. The final payment was in December. With that payment, Bill knew he had no more money coming in. With no money, he couldn't pay the rent, couldn't buy food, and couldn't pay the utility bills. He had no alternative, he thought. He took his own life.

"What a waste," Anthony said. "There were hundreds of alternatives to what he did. He had thirty years to do something, but he never did anything. His parents lived well by working the ranch and at the end they had full ownership of it. As they got older, they really didn't do any work, but they had a great ranch foreman and excellent workers who could have just continued after they died. So, if Bill had kept the working ranch, he could have lived off the profits, forever. Maybe since he had failed at everything, he thought he would fail at that, too. But how do you fail at "doing nothing?"

Julie and Anthony gave many, many hours of their time each week to helping at the local hospital, several local schools, and several retirement homes. They always went together and everyone looked forward to seeing the Adkins.

The hours they donated was nothing compared to the amount of money that they donated to everything in town. It was always an anonymous donation. They never wanted to be recognized for their philanthropic endeavors. They never wanted their name on a hospital wing or in the symphony hall. In addition, they got the most satisfaction of helping people who needed help but had no one to turn to.

When they were driving around one day, they noticed an old house that looked like it hadn't been painted in quite some time. The house looked in disrepair. One shutter was hanging crooked. The wooden steps leading to the house were rotting. They decided to find out who lived there.

Asking the local law enforcement who were frequently in the neighborhood, Anthony found out that Mrs. Richey was an elderly woman who no longer had any family. She lived month to month on her social security checks that weren't enough for her to even replace her television when it broke. She hadn't had a television in years.

"Easy enough," Jonathan thought. *"We are going to take care of this poor woman."*

Julie was excited with this project. Mrs. Richey never saw Julie or Anthony. They sent a crew of painters and handymen to the house to fix everything and to give the house a good coat of paint both inside and outside. Anything that needed to be fixed was. Then, when Anthony's workers told him what the inside looked like-----worn out sofa----little space heater because the heater broke, and no television, he made notes. Anthony and Julie bought new furniture, a television, and new heating and air conditioning. Then Anthony made sure that Mrs. Richey was given a credit card with a credit balance and $1,000 to be added monthly.

At first, Mrs. Richey thought someone was trying to take her home away from her. Even though the workers tried to tell her that they were being paid by someone who just wanted to help her, she didn't believe them. She called the police. It took a lot of work to convince her that it was true----she had been selected to receive these gifts and the donor wanted to remain anonymous. She started crying.

Little did Julie and Anthony know that Mrs. Richey was a very giving person, also. With the extra money that she had been given monthly, she helped other elderly people fix up their homes, or fix their cars, or just get a new television like what happened to her. She paid for their medicine when they couldn't and she helped pay for flowers to brighten up their yards. The generosity shown to Mrs. Richey was passed forward.

4

Julie heard from her teacher friends that there was a young couple who had faced a severe hardship. They had been saving their money doing all kinds of odd jobs to someday buy their own house. Then one of their children became very ill and required very expensive medical treatment. Even with the insurance that they had with their jobs, it wasn't enough. Soon, they had spent every penny that they had saved. When Julie and Anthony found out, they paid for all of the medical expenses and replaced the money they had spent from their savings. In addition, they were notified by a mortgage company that they were given $50,000 to use as a down payment for a new home.

At first, they thought the call was a hoax. They hung up and dismissed the call. Even when the mortgage company sent them a letter explaining the situation, they didn't believe it. *There is a catch,* they thought. It wasn't until they received a statement from the hospital showing that their balance had been paid that they started wondering. Then a mortgage counselor went to their house one evening. He explained that an anonymous donor decided to give them a gift, and it was indeed, legitimate. They couldn't believe it.

Another time, a young woman with three children faced a horrific tragedy. Her husband, a police officer, was killed in the line of duty. Even though there was a small insurance policy, it wasn't enough to take care of the family for long. Julie found out that the mother of the family had wanted to be a teacher, but she quit school to have her first child. She then never went back. Now, she would have to find any job she could find to make ends meet. Julie and Anthony decided to send her enough money each month so that she could go back to school to become a teacher. The amount would be enough to take care of all of their expenses during this time. The money would continue as long as she stayed in school. She also thought it was a hoax. She soon learned that a legitimate anonymous donor wanted to help her out. She started attending classes and became a teacher in a short period of time. She got a job in the same elementary school where her children attended. Because of the help she received, she started helping others with her income. Help doesn't have to be big---just help.

Jonathan and Julie found many, many more cases to take. They got so much satisfaction knowing that they were instrumental in helping people out of their predicaments. *Who can we help now*? They often asked themselves.

Once Anthony and Julie were sitting on the front porch relaxing when a discussion started about tipping. "You know, Julie, you don't have to be wealthy to help others. You don't. You can help others every day by doing little things," he started.

"What little things are you talking about?" Julie inquired.

"Ok, let's say you are an average person with a job," he started explaining. "If you go out to eat, it's customary to tip about 20%. So, if your lunch meal is $10, then the tip would be $2. But what if you tip $3 or $4? It probably wouldn't mean that much to the average worker but it would be HUGE for the waiter or waitress who may be working two jobs to make ends meet. Or what about tipping for a manicure? If you depend on that manicurist and really like the way that person takes care of you, wouldn't it be good to tip more? Or the hairdresser? The point it, for the average person, that little extra amount is going to go unnoticed, but it is huge for the worker who is limited with income. Also, if a person feels he cannot tip any more, what about foregoing that soft drink or that cup of coffee? Why not give the amount you'd spend on your drink as the extra tip? The idea is to give of yourself-----or do you really think you can't make it if you don't get that soft drink. Really? I think people should learn to give more." Then Anthony continued:

"I knew a super wealthy man who played golf at his country club almost every day. He never tipped the ball and bag boys who made sure his clubs were secured on the golf cart and made sure that he had a box of new balls from the club house. They always treated him with utmost respect. Why didn't he give the boys a fifty-dollar bill? Or a hundred-dollar bill? He would have never even noticed! They worked hard for him and would have appreciated it tremendously. Usually, they were high school or college boys who needed extra money for their car repair or college tuition."

Anthony practiced what he preached---giving greatly appreciated tips to everyone he knew.

7

"Remember Julie, you don't have to be wealthy to do really nice things for other people. There is a really nice lady that I know named Margaret who did something really nice for disadvantaged children at Christmas time. I don't know how much money she set aside for this activity, but she took that money and bought toys and clothes to give to children who were from the poorer neighborhoods. To these children, a new toy was something to really get excited about. She enjoyed this activity so much that she continued it for many years. As far as I know, she is still doing it!

You see, if people would just step out and do something nice for someone else, they would see the benefit that they receive for themselves. They would receive more than what they would give. It just works that way." Anthony wondered how he could get others to understand that message.

Chapter 22
Julie's Other Passion

Anthony and Julie spent most of their time volunteering around town. But when they weren't, Julie loved to read and study about vitamins, minerals, hormones, and nutrients. Her mother had always been a big believer in adding supplements to one's diet to maintain good health. It must have rubbed off on Julie.

One day when Anthony and Julie were talking about his difficulty with acid reflux, she grabbed a couple of her books and started reading on the subject. She found out that there is a big controversary concerning acid reflux. One train of thought, the conventional medical model, states that acid reflux occurs when one has too much acid in the stomach, thus causing severe pain. The doctors generally prescribe acid blockers which work to stop the production of acid in the stomach lining. The acid blockers prescribed were never intended to be used for longer than a six-month period of time, but most people stay on them indefinitely.

In contrast to that was of thinking, the homeopathic doctors believe that acid reflux actually occurs when a person gets older and is no longer producing acid like before. Therefore, instead of producing too much acid, the stomach is producing too little acid, causing the food to become putrefied in the stomach. The putrefaction of food due to not enough stomach acid as one ages causes gas to form, causing bubbles to sometimes push partially digested food mixed with stomach acid up into the esophagus, causing burping and a painful burning sensation----thus heart burn.

There is one way to absolutely find out if a person has too much stomach acid or not enough, but it entails a test capsule lowered into the stomach and then retrieved with the acid results. That test is rarely done. It is so much easier to just prescribe an acid blocker to relieve the pain. The patient is happy not knowing that he is setting himself up for other more serious problems later in life. There may be some cases where a particular disease leaves the patient no choice. But, generally, a person with acid reflux or heart burn has the difficulty because of too little stomach acid.

What happens if a person doesn't have enough stomach acid? If there is too little acid, any food eaten will not fully digest so the vitamins and nutrients in the food will not be processed and absorbed by the body. The person is eating, but the body is not receiving what it needs to continue rebuilding tissue where and when needed. In essence, the body is being starved of what it needs. Then tissues and systems start breaking down over time.

When Anthony had problems after he ate with acid reflux and heart burn, he went to a great gastroenterologist who prescribed a common acid blocker. After Julie read about taking hydrochloric acid, he tried that. He also loved apple cider vinegar. He could drink it right out of a glass. I guess that was his body telling him that he needed more acid. Julie also remembered that her grandmother used to squeeze a whole lemon into a glass of water after every meal. She was, in fact, putting more acid into her stomach. It worked; she had no acid reflux. *Do you know of anything a person has that works better or that you have more of as one ages?* Julie thought.

Anthony had difficulty with his knees so much that he made an appointment with one of the top orthopedic surgeons. Anthony had played a lot of sports, particularly tennis, and his knee joints were worn out. He had surgery to 'scope' both knees. That procedure entailed cutting away the frayed meniscus or cleaning it up to be smooth. The procedure was very successful and Anthony enjoyed pain free knees for almost twelve years. Then his knees started hurting all over again.

This time, Julie went with Anthony when he had his doctor's visit. "Doc, I'm back to use my warranty. I think I'm gonna have to have knee surgery again. I'm sure you gave me a guarantee last time, didn't ya? It's only been twelve years," Anthony said with a dead serious look on his face. Dr. McCullough laughed. He knew Anthony.

Then Dr. McCullough offered some excellent advice after he did x-rays. "Anthony, if you'd just take some glucosamine, you wouldn't have to have your knees scoped. Just start taking it every day and you'll be fine. Oh, you might get a floater once in a while, but that's nothing. I get those, too. I'll hobble around here for a couple of days, and then the particle that is causing the problem will lodge somewhere behind my knee and I'm good to go."

Julie was taking all his advice in. She had been very athletic growing up and played many sports. Her knees were worn out also. She didn't have to have them scoped but she had floaters on more than one occasion and it was pretty debilitating. Both Anthony and Julie started talking glucosamine capsules regularly. Then, when Julie got into her sixties, she started having pretty strong pain in her right knee and also her right hip.

"Anthony," she said, "I'm having pain in my knee and my hip. It's affecting the way I'm walking." She actually thought that she was on her way to a knee replacement like her mother had.

Anthony suggested that she double up on her glucosamine intake. She did, and within days, the pain in her knee and hip had disappeared. *I don't know why I didn't think of that!*

"What other supplements do you recommend?" Anthony asked her one day when they had a discussion on their health.

"Ya know, I asked the nice lady in the vitamin store if she could recommend something for my brain. I was taking supplements for every other part of my body so why not the brain?" Julie answered. "The lady told me to take phosphatidylserine. It is a natural substance that your brain is made up of anyway. So, I bought a bottle and started taking the capsules as directed. I really didn't think I would be able to tell anything, but then something interesting happened. I was gardening in the backyard when I heard a dog bark in the forested area behind the house. The dog bark made a memory jump into my head from sixty years earlier. When I was in junior high school, I wanted a poodle puppy. I asked my mother if I could get one and she replied that she knew of a lady in town who raised puppies. Her name was Robbie Tharp. Now, when you are a young kid and you are going to pick up a cute, little poodle puppy, do you really care about what the ladies name is? Plus, I was *terrible* with names and always have been. That name--- Robbie Tharp---jumped into my head like it was yesterday. I'm sure I only heard her name two or three times over sixty years ago! It had to be the phosphatidylserine. On another occasion, someone mentioned the importance of teachers and another name popped into my head from when I was in college. A fellow classmate who sat next to me mentioned that a school can run without administrators for a while, but that a school cannot run for one hour without teachers. His name was Jack Barton. He was not a close friend but merely an acquaintance in that class. I had not thought about him since finishing that class yet his name popped into my head instantly. I also found that other areas of my life improved because of the enhanced organization phosphatidylserine provided. For example, every year when I cooked Thanksgiving dinner, I felt rushed and stressed to get everything done on time. After taking phosphatidylserine, I found that it took much less time, although the menu was exactly the same. The difference was that I was not retracing my steps as often; I was more organized," Julie explained.

Anthony was fascinated. He asked, "Did you give this supplement to anyone else?"

"Yes, since phosphatidylserine evidently made a significant impact on my memory, I decided to buy some for my mother. After taking the supplement for two weeks she promptly stopped. She quit because she was reliving childhood conversations that she had with her own mother. The conversations were disturbing and she never wanted to relive them. I explained that she should remain on the capsules because it would level out as her brain adapted. She refused," Julie answered.

"Another interesting point," Julie continued. "I found out that phosphatidylserine is used as a natural ADHD medicine for children and is sometimes given to people with Alzheimer's Disease. Since phosphatidylserine diminishes as a person ages, it is important to give the brain what it needs to keep functioning properly."

"You mentioned that Alek took ADHD medication. Did you try phosphatidylserine first?" Anthony asked.

"No, I didn't know about it at that time. But, even now, I believe the medication works faster and better. I think the phosphatidylserine takes a lot longer and is not as effective as medication for children who have ADHD," Julie answered.

"OK, what other miracle supplements are up your sleeve?" Anthony said as he hugged Julie affectionately.

"Oh, goodness. There's vitamin D3, vitamin C, vitamin A, selenium, melatonin,......I can go on and on," Julie answered. She loved talking about supplements because she felt they were very good for improving health. In fact, she felt that as a person ages, it's mandatory to give one's body the necessary vitamins, minerals, and nutrients to rebuild tissues that break down with age.

"Go ahead and tell me, Julie. I may need some help," Anthony laughed. "I'm really interested in everything you're saying."

"Anthony, did you know that garlic was like a medicine in ancient Egyptian times?" Anthony looked at Julie with a puzzled look on his face. "Yes, in ancient times, people bathed but also drank water from the Nile River. They did everything in the Nile including going to the 'restroom' there! So obviously when someone had a stomach virus or diarrhea it would run rampant through the village. The one thing that would cure their intestinal problems was garlic. So, today with easy supplements, it's easy to ward off intestinal problems with garlic capsules."

Then Julie continued since she had a captive and interested audience, "Did you know that many eye problems can be improved with supplements? I had a close friend whose father lost his vision at a young age. She started developing macular degeneration also and feared she, too, would suffer his same fate, so she went to the ophthalmologist for help. He placed her on several supplements for eye health. She took lutein, zeaxanthin, copper, omega-3, DHA, EPA, vitamin C and E, and zinc. Since her situation was serious, her doctor asked her to take more than the normal amount. To this day, her eyesight is fine. Without the supplements, would she have lost her sight like her father did?"

Julie took a little pause in her lecture but noticing that Anthony was still listening and appeared to be interested, she went on. "Is it common that most older people have a hearing loss?" she asked. "Well, with the proper supplements to rebuild the inner ear, those people don't have to have a loss of hearing. I'm not saying it works every single time, because sometimes hearing loss is due to many other things, but it does work much of the time. Vitamin B12 deficiency can actually cause the deterioration of the neurons in the cochlear nerve, causing a hearing loss. Magnesium and zinc are also important for hearing. Anthony, we both need to be taking a good multi vitamin that includes all of these things---just to cover everything."

"No one ever thinks of this, do they? I mean, we all get older, so we just naturally think we are supposed to lose our hearing, lose our memory, experience joint pain, lose our eyesight…..all of that. How would anyone know that these can be prevented to some extent? Not everyone reads all the books like you do," Anthony mentioned.

"I only have one more thing to tell you. If I don't stop, I'll keep talking til midnight!" Julie said as if she were rushing to get one more piece of important information out. "Hormones are extremely important. When your hormones are gone, you are on your way out. When you age, your hormones decline. Practically everything that happens to a person after the age of forty is caused by hormones declining. For example, adult diabetes, heart attacks, Parkinson's Disease, coronary artery disease, dementia, Alzheimer's disease, and any cancers just to name a few. I've even read an article by a Dr. Riegel who said that 90% of breast cancers and prostate cancers have been linked to low hormones. You can do something about that! It's easy!"

"Ok, Julie. Just tell me what to take and where to buy it!" Anthony said sounding somewhat exhausted. "I can't be a walking encyclopedia of information like you!" *Plus, I'm not reading all that stuff,* he thought.

Chapter 23
Surprise at the End

It was time to give up the mini ranch. With all of their philanthropic and volunteer activities, Jonathan and Julie wanted to be closer to the hospitals and schools. The animals, ducks, and fish had long passed away and were never replaced. Andrew and Cassie were grown with children of their own who were also almost grown and out of the house.

After the mini ranch sold, they took one more walk around the property to relive old memories. "Julie, do you remember how surprised you were to first see this house? I think you really loved the inside but when you first saw this backyard and saw the animals, I could see the excitement in your eyes." Jonathan said as he held her close.

"Oh, are you kidding? I couldn't believe it! First, I looked at the pool, and of course, who could get past the kids screaming! But then, I saw this animal pen beyond the pool, and I immediately fell in love with it. I actually thought the people who were selling the house still owned the animals. I didn't know until you told me later, that you had bought them at the local feed store. The animals were so precious. We had many good times with those little creatures, didn't we!" Julie reminisced.

"And what about the koi pond?" Anthony added.

"That was another dream come true. To have large fish eating out of Cassie's and Drew's hands was quite special," Julie answered. "And what about when it snowed and the kids----and you----sledded down the slope on the side of the house on garbage can lids?"

"I have to admit it really was fun. Then there were several times when we were able to build a snowman. I think they got better as we became more experienced. We have several great pictures of our snowmen," Anthony said. "And the snow ice cream, and the Christmas times and the decorations. I could go on and on."

Their final tour of the premises was a nice conclusion to a wonderful life on the mini ranch and a nice review of the great times they shared there with their family. *Say goodbye*, Anthony said to himself sadly.

2

It was time to slow down. They continued giving money to needy people and enjoyed every minute of it. They never wanted to be recognized. They never wanted their name on a building. They preferred to remain anonymous.

One evening when Julie and Anthony were talking, he explained that they were in the winter of their lives. "Tell me your thoughts, Anthony," Julie said knowing he was going to tell her anyway.

"Well, when we first met, we were in the early spring of our lives together. We were just starting to peek our heads up out of the ground like flowers do in the spring. Our relationship was just 'budding.' Then, as our relationship grew, we were in the 'Spring' time of our relationship. Everything was so beautiful. Flowers were everywhere----the grass was a vivid green----life was so perfect. Then our relationship went into the beginnings of summer. We were apart from each other----you raised our son and taught school and then welcomed grandchildren into your life. I married, had a successful career but a disappointing marriage, and then a separation. So, we missed most of Summer together. By the end of Summer, we found each other again. We raised our grandchildren as our own, and we had the life together that we had always wanted. We had the most amazing and most incredible life together raising Andrew and Cassie. As they grew up, and we got older, we entered the Fall of our lives. We slowed down, somewhat, but enjoyed the volunteering and philanthropy part of living. The leaves of the trees fell at the end of our Fall relationship. Then our Winter relationship started. We slowed down even more but still enjoyed each other's company so much that we didn't need any other entertainment. We enjoyed just sitting and talking. Now, we are at the end of our Winter lives. We are facing medical issues, but life is still very good. We need to enjoy our Winter, Julie, because there will be no more Spring."

Julie knew exactly what Anthony meant. They were coming to the end of their lives.

3

It was just as Anthony had pointed out. They were both getting older, and their health was slowly failing. Julie couldn't remember things as well as before. She credited her failing memory to just old age. She never drove any more, instead leaving it up to Anthony; she was afraid she would not remember how to get back home, if she drove somewhere. She couldn't remember the names of some of her best friends. Once when she and Anthony arrived home, she took off her coat and then tried to hang it in the hall closet. She couldn't remember where the closet was. She opened a door, but it was the hall bathroom. Tears streamed down her face.

After things started happening that seemed well beyond the norm, Anthony took Julie to the doctor. A brain tumor had gone undetected, and then it started affecting Julie's balance. She could no longer walk. Over time, she declined more and more. Jonathan stayed by her bed almost every minute of every day. He also hired a fulltime nurse to take care of her and to fulfill all of her needs.

Anthony watched as Julie declined steadily. He knew that she loved reading the newspaper and she made a daily routine of doing it. Then, she slowly started reading less and less. One day, Anthony held the newspaper up in front of her eyes, so she could read it easier; she had difficulty holding the paper up. Julie looked up at the paper, but her eyes weren't connecting with the words. It's as if she couldn't read any longer. She glanced around the page just like a baby would—looking at the pictures but not making connection with any words. Anthony knew her brain was deteriorating. The brain tumor was taking over her faculties. She spoke less and less. She only answered with "uh-huh" and "no." She never asked any questions; she never asked for anything. She slept all of the time.

When Julie wasn't asleep, it appeared that she was talking to her deceased relatives. Anthony watched as she whispered things to someone who was clearly not in the bedroom. "Mom?" Julie asked one day as she looked up toward the ceiling.

"Julie, darling, do you see your mother?" Anthony asked very seriously.

"She's there," Julie answered then closed her eyes.

Anthony knew that sometimes when a person is near the end of life, the person will see and even talk to loved ones who have passed before. Anthony's Aunt Stella told him that when his uncle, her husband, was near the end of his life, he talked to his dead family members frequently. When she asked him one day who he was talking to, he acted irritated. "Well, John and William…can't you see?" he responded.

Anthony remembered his Aunt Stella telling him, "Sometime after Al died, I was awakened in the middle of the night. I had fallen asleep in his recliner in front of the television set. Something kicked the chair or something jarred me awake. I opened my eyes and saw Al standing right in front of me as clear as day. He had his plaid pajamas on, and his arms were crossed in front of him. He was in front of the television. I know I was awake. As soon as I saw him, he disappeared. But, I will never, ever forget it."

One cold, winter evening, Julie couldn't fight any longer. She told Anthony it was time for her to go. "I've gotta go now," she whispered. He looked at her with a puzzled look on his face. *She hasn't spoken that much in weeks*, he thought. Then she squeezed his hand and closed her eyes. He watched as she took her last breath. He kissed her hand, leaned over to her face to kiss her on the cheek, then sat back to just stare at her. He loved her so much. He had lost her, again. He thanked God for the wonderful life they had for the past fifty years. Their life was better than what most people had, even though they missed out on so many years in the beginning.

Anthony waited before he called hospice. He had been instructed to call hospice first and the hospice nurse would take care of everything else for him. He waited to call, because he knew Julie would be taken away, and he wasn't ready. He just wasn't

198

ready. *Let me be with her just a little longer,* he prayed.

When the hospice nurse came, she handed Anthony a letter that Julie had written. Many months ago, Julie had given the letter to the nurse with directions to give it to Anthony after her death. "Mr. Adkins, your beloved Julie wrote this letter and wanted me to give it you after she passed."

Anthony opened the envelope and slowly pulled out the letter:

My Dearest Anthony,

If you are reading this, then I am no longer with you. But, Anthony, you are in my heart. You gave me the most beautiful life that any person could ever have. Even though we were kept apart early on, it didn't matter once we were back together again. It was like we didn't miss one day. We had beautiful children to raise as our very own and we experienced more than most parents. My only regret is that you never got to meet your son. More of a regret is that he never got to meet you. I can never forgive myself for that. Our later years were filled with the wonderful experiences of helping others. Our lives were enriched because of that. Now that I have come to the end of my life, I want you to know how thankful I am that we were together. Better yet, I know that we will be together again.....I promise. And don't forget....I will love you forever.

I Love You,
Julie

Anthony noticed that she had taped three pennies to the bottom of the letter. *Of course, she did*, he whispered.

4

Anthony, Cassie, and Andrew discussed Julie's end of life wishes. She had always told Anthony that she wanted to be cremated. She taught a high school summer school class one time and her assignment topic was "Death and Dying." The book used for the class was titled "On Death and Dying" by Elisabeth Kubler-Ross. She arranged a field trip to a crematorium for her students. The gentleman there explained how bodies were cremated and even took the students into the room where bodies were prepared after death. He explained the process in detail. After that field trip, Julie never wanted to be buried in a coffin. She insisted on being cremated and her ashes scattered. She often said, "Let my ashes dance and play one more time, before they float away."

She told Cassie that she preferred donating part of her body to help someone else if possible. "If I am *so old* that there is nothing worth saving or donating, then just donate my body to be used as a cadaver for the medical school. Then when they call to ask if you want my ashes, just tell them to throw them away. What are ashes anyway?" Julie told

Cassie and Anthony that they could make the decision based on what they really wanted to do, but if it were up to her, she would say, "No life support, no obituary, no embalming, just cremation, no grave site, no headstone, and no funeral." She often said, "Just let me go quietly into the night."

After almost all of Julie's wishes were fulfilled, and a small, intimate family gathering gave her a send-off, Cassie begged her father to move in with her and her family. He finally agreed and started working on his house every day to clean out everything. Cassie helped him. They donated the furniture and everything in the house that Cassie and Andrew and their children could no longer use.

"Dad, we have just about everything taken care of in the house," Cassie said one morning. "I just need you to go through that old trunk that Mom had in the guest bedroom. It's full of things that were important to her. Let's decide what we want to keep and what we can donate."

He agreed to go and they drove down the street to his house. It was difficult for Anthony to see the house, knowing that Julie died there. His mind was flooded with emotions. He and Cassie worked for a few minutes in the kitchen when she told him she needed to go meet a client. It would only take about an hour and then she would be back to help him with the trunk.

"Sure, Cassie----you go ahead. I'll be fine," he said feeling like he could handle it without her. He finished what he wanted to do in the kitchen and then walked into the guest bedroom. The old trunk had been with Julie long before he and Julie married. The trunk was a rather large, wooden trunk with tarnished brass hardware. The top was rounded with decorative leather straps across it, fastened with brass tacks. The lock was still a workable lock, but Julie never turned the key to lock it. The contents were very valuable to her, but she didn't think anyone else would find them to be valuable. Anthony knew she kept keepsakes in it, but never opened it.

He raised the lid and sat in a chair next to it. The first thing he saw was a painting that Julie had done many, many years earlier, when their son was very young. The painting was a typical family portrait with Anthony, Julie, and little Alek. As he stared at it, he realized: *We weren't together when Alek was little. I never saw Alek. I guess Julie painted this painting because this is how it should have been. I should have been right there---like in this picture. I should have been father to Alek.* His heart broke. He had never seen the painting. Julie had never mentioned it.

Then Anthony saw the ring that he had given her when she was only seventeen years old. It was plastic and had an enormous 'diamond' in the center. He had given it to her on one of their outings that summer. He never dreamed that she would have kept that silly thing after all of these years. What he didn't realize is that it wasn't silly to her. *It wasn't silly.* She had tied it to the side of the trunk with a piece of satin ribbon.

Then Anthony saw a couple of handmade afghans that Julie had crocheted before arthritis made the hobby too difficult to do. She loved sitting in her favorite chair, watching television, while she crocheted. It was so fulfilling to her when she finally finished an afghan and then gave it to someone. It took an average of fifty hours to crochet just one; it was truly an act of love. Anthony saw the scrap book with all of Alek's honors and awards--- and his Boy Scout certificates. I know Julie was extremely proud of Alek. He tried to visualize being at the awards ceremony where Alek would have gotten his new merit badges. He would have been that extremely proud father. Just one more thing he missed out on.

He also saw several items from Alek's early childhood. Julie saved his favorite stuffed animal— a teddy bear with a faded red shirt. All faded and worn, Anthony imagined what it would have been like to see little Alek toddling around, carrying his favorite teddy bear. Anthony tried to relive that moment. He also found the first truck that Alek must have had. It was carved out of wood, but the paint had scraped off. The paint that remained chipped off as he lifted it. There was a string on one end. He could see Alek toddling through the kitchen, pulling the little wooden truck behind him.

Anthony tried to picture being there. *I missed out on so much,* he thought.

Carefully tucked on the side of the trunk was a small sack. When Anthony opened it, he saw that it contained a small plastic reindeer with red eyes. He could tell it was very, very old. Then he remembered that when Julie was a small child, there was a plastic reindeer with red eyes that her family always put out at Christmas time. She looked forward to seeing the reindeer each Christmas. He didn't know for sure, but he thought Julie told him it was a gift from Julie's father to her and her sister when they were young. They each got one; they cost ten cents each. Julie thought it had been lost for many, many years, and then it suddenly appeared when her mother was in her eighties. Julie was thrilled. If Anthony was right about the story, then the reindeer would be somewhere around one hundred years old. No wonder Julie kept it in her beloved trunk.

Anthony also saw a small basket. The basket was a gift from a cousin to Julie's grandmother when her mother was born. It arrived in the mail, unwrapped with just a ribbon and tag tied on the handle with the address. It arrived undamaged. Julie knew she had to identify the basket with a tag since no one would ever know how old it was. Anyone else would have thrown out that basket not knowing the sentimental value.

Just as Anthony was finished looking though the items, and when he was lowering the lid of the trunk, he noticed a piece of paper barely sticking out of a slit in the lining in the top of the trunk. It turned out to be a large manila envelope.

What is this? This was placed just where no one would see this, he said to himself. It was clear that the slit in the lining was done purposely and the envelope was slid inside to hide it. It could have easily gone undetected forever.

He opened the old, brittle envelope. He slowly slid the papers out of the envelope. Pulling out the papers, he read:

Connecticut University Hospital
Organ Donation Program

The papers were informative sheets and legal documents explaining the hospital's organ donor program. The date on the document was April 8, 1952. That was a few days before Anthony's kidney surgery. As he read further, he noticed the section where a signature was notarized. The name Julie Johnson was signed on the signature line. The section asking for the donor's wishes to remain anonymous was checked and signed. *Julie didn't want me to know.*

Then another document notified Julie of the date of the surgery to donate her kidney. The date was April 13, 1952----the *exact date* that Anthony received his kidney. *The exact date........*

6

Back in 1952, Julie heard that Anthony was in critical condition. Even though she thought he was happily married, and she tried to get him out of her mind, when she heard that he needed a kidney transplant, she couldn't think of anything else. She didn't hesitate. She knew she had to at least go through the testing to determine if she were an acceptable donor or not.

First, she talked to her parents. She explained what she wanted to do. "Mom, Dad, I don't know if you have heard, but Anthony was in a terrible accident, and he is in critical condition. The accident didn't kill him, but he lost one kidney right away, and the other one started shutting down. They put him on dialysis, but he didn't respond to that treatment very well. His doctors are afraid he is going to die if someone doesn't donate a kidney. I still love him, and I want to be tested to see if I would be able to be a donor." She looked at her parents and tried to read their expression.

Their hearts were heavy. "Julie, are you sure you want to do this? What if you have medical difficulties later in life and cannot function with only one kidney? You need to think of yourself, too. Or what Alek. What if Alek needed a kidney sometime?" They didn't think too much of it, because they really didn't believe she would be a donor match. After all, the chance of being a donor match to Anthony had to be extremely small.

"I have to do this. I just want to be tested to know that I have done everything I could do. Even if it doesn't work out, I know I tried," she rationalized.

She immediately scheduled an appointment at the donor clinic and had the necessary blood and tissue tests for donor compatibility. She had to go in for additional testing as the program stated. Every time she was tested, she felt better and better about what she was doing. *I may not be an acceptable donor for Anthony, but at least I know that I did what I could possibly do to help him. He's the father of my son. I will always love him.*

After a few weeks, Julie was notified by a phone call that she was a compatible donor. "Ms. Johnson, this is Dr. Moran with the organ donor program. I want to personally thank you offering to be a donor. We have tested your blood and tissue to determine compatibility and it is perfect for your friend, Anthony Adkins. In fact, you are a better match than we even hoped for. Do you have any questions?" the doctor said.

"I'm sure I'll have questions as I think about this more, but for now, I don't think I have any," she replied feeling good about the entire process. "I just want to make sure I'm an anonymous donor."

"Absolutely. We have your signature notarized and we *will* abide by your wishes," he reiterated.

With the properly notarized paperwork, she was scheduled for surgery. She donated her kidney on the same day that Anthony received it. Their surgeries were on the same day; it was orchestrated perfectly.

On the day of surgery, the sun shone brightly and the clouds in the sky looked beautiful and soft. The trees were starting to bud out, and grass was starting to turn green. Spring is the time for new growth and the time for re-birth. *This is appropriate* she thought. *This is the spring in Anthony's new life.* Everything was good. Julie's parents were very supportive. They could see how much it meant to Julie to donate her kidney to Anthony. Even though they were fearful inside, they never showed it.

Julie had no fear or anxiety. She never thought twice about donating her kidney to give Anthony a normal life. She just didn't want him to know she was the donor. She didn't want him to feel obligated to her or to feel that he owed her anything. It would be fine, in her mind, to remain anonymous. In fact, she remained anonymous even until the day that she died.

All of these years, Anthony never knew it was Julie
who had donated her life-saving kidney. He never
even suspected it. He couldn't believe it. She
saved his life.

Sitting beside the old trunk, he stared at the papers
for a few minutes then carefully put them back into
the envelope. He walked out of the bedroom, past
the kitchen, to the closet in his office. He picked up
a red Folgers coffee can that had been sitting on his
shelf in his office closet for many years and walked
to the coat rack where his coat and scarf hung.
Setting down the coffee can, he put on his coat,
slung the scarf around his neck, picked up the can,
and walked out the back door.

The weather turned cold; the sky was overcast and
dark clouds loomed in the distance. Wind whipped
around the trees, blowing leaves down the street and
making a whining sound that was ominous. Holding
his scarf close to his face, Anthony walked three
blocks very slowly and wondered if he could even
make it. He hadn't walked more than a few yards in
quite some time. In addition, the Folgers can was
quite heavy---very heavy---heavier than he thought
it would be. It was full of pennies. He collected
every penny that Julie gave him over the years.

He finally made it to the corner and then walked
through the carved wrought iron gate into the
cemetery where the ashes of his beloved Julie were

buried. He walked up to her headstone, lay the crinkled envelope on her grave and anchored it with his red Folgers coffee can so it wouldn't blow off. He told Julie, "We will be together again......I promise." Then he turned to walk away.

After three steps, he turned back around and dug his right hand into his pants pocket. The coins jingled. He pulled out his change. He had a variety of coins, but he picked out four pennies. He placed the pennies heads-up on Julie's headstone. Then Anthony hobbled over to the wrought-iron bench about twenty feet from her grave and sat down. He pulled the scarf closer to his face to stave off the cold wind. He stared at the name on her headstone: *Julie Michelle Johnson* Memories flooded his mind.

Julie and I were so much in love. We were meant to be together from the very beginning, but our relationship was sabotaged, and we didn't even know it was happening. Our lives went two separate ways. I married and led a life I never really wanted. I became very successful in my career, but was it worth it? Money can't buy happiness. It just can't. Julie had our son and spent her life caring for him. She was a wonderful mother. They had a happy life but then the accident happened. Alek and his wife were so young when they died. Julie took the children to be their mother and father, but then we found each other again. From that day forward, we had the most beautiful life anyone could ever have. Financial independence gave us both the time to be with the children every single day, all day long. I finally had the children I had wanted all of my life. After the children grew up, Julie and I enjoyed being together every minute of every day. We were blessed to be able to make other people happy. Now, she has been taken from me again. I'm glad my time is limited here on earth.

Then Anthony said one more time like he had said numerous times over the years… "We will be together again…..I promise."

8

Cassie finished with her client meeting and headed back to the house. She, too, noticed the weather turning colder and the wind whipping around. As she drove home, she was thankful that her father was able to go back to the house he and Julie shared together and that he had the strength to face the many memories stored in the old trunk.

Walking through the back door, she noticed her father's coat and scarf were not hanging on the coat rack. "Dad?" she called out. "Dad?" She got no answer. She ran to the guest bedroom, but he was not there. The lid was open on the trunk, so he had clearly been working on its contents. He was not in his office, either. *I can't believe he'd go out. He never ventures out anymore. And it's so cold!* Then she had a thought on where he might be. She raced out of the house and jumped back into the car. She drove the three blocks to the cemetery, jumped out of the car and ran through the gate. "Dad?" she cried out. "Dad?"

She ran past her mother's headstone and noticed the red coffee can on top of the grave. She looked over towards the bench and there was her father, bundled up in his coat and scarf----slumped over.

"Dad!" she yelled as she ran to him.

He kept his promise.

The End

Author's Personal Notes

Many of the names, dates, and events in this book are from the author's actual life. The following is a list of those items for the reader's interest.

1. Julie is the name of a personal friend. (p.1)
2. Gloria is the name of a personal friend. (p.1)
3. Randell is the name of the author's brother. (p.1)
4. The author's father didn't believe in insurance. (p. 1)
5. The author's father was quite a handyman. (p.1)
6. The Dairy Queen is the name of the teen hangout when the author was a teenager. (p.2)
7. Mary is the name of a personal friend. (p.5)
8. Anthony is the name of the author's nephew. (p.8)
9. Johnson is the author's maiden name. (p.7)
10. Adkins is the last name of the author's friends. (p.18)
11. Lubbock County is the county where the
12. author was born. (p.20)
13. Childhood memories are true incidents in
14. the author's life. (p.25-)
13. Dr. Jaynes was the author's doctor. (p. 30)
14. Debbie is the name of the author's best

friend in high school. (p.33)

15. Brandon was the father of the author's best friend. (p. 48)

16. The incident with the crescent rolls was true. (p. 48)

15. Bradfield is the name of an elementary school where the author worked. (p.50)

16. Gena is the name of the author's friend. (p.51)

17. Albert is the name of the author's husband. (p.54)

18. Marilyn is the name of a personal friend. (p.56)

19. Moran is the last name of the author's friends. (p.71)

20. Burton is the last name of the author's friend. (p.74)

21. The number 13 stories are true stories for the author. (p.75)

22. The hallucinations are real stories based on the author's brother. (p.82)

23. Alek is the name of the author's nephew. (p.87)

24. Playing school was in the author's childhood. (p.88)

25. Stories on reading and phonics were true about author's daughter. (p.88)

26. The author's daughter read sentences two weeks before turning three. (p.88)

27. Stories on page 89-93 were true of the author's daughter. (p. 89-93)

28. Pickrel is the married name for the author's daughter. (p.94)

29. Story of the ADHD student is a true story of the author's student. (p. 94)
30. Andrew is the name of the author's nephew (p.98)
31. The author took art classes at a Hobby Lobby. (98)
32. Calonnie was the author's art teacher. (p.99)
33. The story about art was true for the author. (p.99)
34. Joseph is the name of the author's brother-in-law. (p.99)
35. Cathy is the name of the author's friend. (p.104)
36. Cassie is the daughter of a friend of the author. (p.105)
37. Mimi is the name the author's nephew calls his grandmother. (p.119)
38. January 5 is the birthday of a close friend. (p.)
39. Drewsy is the nickname of the author's nephew. (p.124)
40. The author had a mini horse, two pigmy goats, numerous rabbits and ducks along with dogs and cats. (p.136)
41. Arnold is the name of the author's brother-in-law. (p.134)
42. Author had goats named Annabell and Billy. (p.137)
43. Author had a mini horse named Bo. (p.140)
44. The author had ducks and many rabbits. (p. 142)
45. The author's mini horse lost a tooth. (p.142)

46. Neighbors brought rabbits to the author when they found them. (p.143)
47. The author adopted a schnauzer named Randolf from friend Betty. (p.144)
48. The author had a Doberman and a cat. (p.144)
49. The story about handing over the dog was true. (p.145)
51. 'Hang on, Annabell' is a true story. (p.146)
52. The stories of the counselor's testing were true. (p.149)
53. Catherine is the name of the author's niece. (p.149)
54. The author played basketball, volleyball, tennis and track. (p.160)
55. The author took piano lessons and twirling lessons. (p.150)
56. The story of cookie decorating was true except for senior center (p.154)
57. Decorating Styrofoam balls was a true story for the author. (p.156)
58. The story of golf was true. (p.160)
59. The stories of being late were true. (p.160)
60. The story of the working ranch and Bill was true. (p.168)
61. Bill is the name of the author's friend. (p.169)
62. Richey is the last name of the author's friend. (p.171)
63. The story of the wealthy golfer not tipping is true. (p.176)
64. The author loves reading about supplements. (p. 178)

65. Supplement information and stories are true. (p.178)
66. The story about Margaret, friend of the author, is true. (p.176)
67. Dr. McCullough was author's doctor; name of middle school (p.180)
68. Stella is the name of the author's friend. (p.192)
69. Story of Uncle Al talking to deceased relatives is true. (p.192)
70. The author taught a course on death and dying. (p.195)
71. The author crochets afghans. (p.198)
72. The plastic reindeer is a real story. (p.199)
73. April 8 is the author's husband's birthday. (p.200)
74. April 13 is the author's birthday. (p. 201)
75. Michelle is the middle name of the author's daughter. (p. 205)

Made in the USA
Middletown, DE
20 July 2019